છ

It Happens To Them Sometimes

and other stories

To Dave Wrey
Thanks for the drinking,
cursing and womanizing!

Cheers
Vincent
J.F.C.

It Happens To Them Sometimes

and other stories

Vincent Sperando

Pentland Press, Inc.
England • USA • Scotland

PUBLISHED BY PENTLAND PRESS, INC.
5124 Bur Oak Circle, Raleigh, North Carolina 27612
United States of America
919-782-0281

ISBN 1-57197-048-7
Library of Congress Catalog Card Number 96-71764

Cover design by Dina Sperando

Printed in the United States of America

For Frances Marie Sperando

ॐ

Acknowledgments

I would like to express gratitude to everyone who didn't scoff at me when I told them I was going to write. With special thanks to everyone who encouraged and assisted me along the long path to publication. In chronological order, I would like to thank my entire family, Joseph P. Fawcett, Paul Stern, Doris Jean Austin and especially my wife Deborah de Fina who has been with me since the first page.

I would also like to thank my sister, Dina Sperando, for designing such a beautiful cover.

ℰꝺ

Contents

ॐ

*It Happens to
Them Sometimes*

F OR THE FIFTH OCCASION IN A YEAR'S TIME, Dominic Direnzo went to his closet and retrieved the gray garment bag that contained his most formal suit. He wished it was the last time he'd need to wear the Calvin Klein designer suit, but there were two more formal events scheduled for the summer and always something unexpected happening in Rosewood, the small town where he had spent his entire life. Rosewood was a socially active town, just west of the city, and much like the many neighborhoods east of it but with its own mayor and police force. Dominic Direnzo was being optimistic when he figured he'd only need to wear the suit three more times.

As always he tossed the garment bag onto his bed, unzipped it, and inspected the suit inside for any imperfections. There were none. It was perfectly black. So black that the absence of color dazed him for a moment because it appeared there was nothing in front of him. There were no shades of color and no perception of depth which took on the appearance of infinite depth where he was lost somewhere.

His friend Frank Spano stood behind him in the bedroom and asked, "You alright?"

He jolted. ". . . Yeah, I'm fine."

"Is the suit alright?"

"Yeah."

"Then put it on. What are you waitin' for? I wanna get goin'."

"I was thinkin'," Dominic Direnzo said. "It seems our friends are either dying or gettin' married."

"Well, you have to do at least one of the two. And almost everyone in this town'll do both."

"Don't joke about it."

"Why not?" Frank Spano asked. "What's buggin' you, anyway?"

"Peppi Bardutti, that's what. You haven't forgot his wake, have ya?"

"No, Dom, I haven't. Who could?"

It was an enormous wake that took place the previous month on the 5th and 6th of April. Everyone from Rosewood went.

"But he wasn't one of us," Frank Spano continued.

"We're all from the same town."

"But they don't hang with us."

"We play softball with them."

"Against them."

"We're still from the same town. We have to stick together. You want the niggers and spicks to take over? What's wrong with you, Stumpy?"

Frank Spano, or Stumpy as he was known because of his bulldog frame, didn't answer. He didn't care who lived in Rosewood. His friends were his friends and he didn't think much about anyone else. He only formed opinions about those close to him. He thought Dominic Direnzo was too old-fashioned but loved him anyway because he depended on him and trusted him as he trusted himself. They were as close as brothers. They did everything together.

At Peppi Bardutti's wake, they hung together in the back of Perazzo's Funeral Home while certain other kids their age

2

stood up front near the casket. That's the way it was in Rosewood. Peppi Bardutti's closer friends were treated like family. Most everyone else was there to give the impression of respect.

When Stumpy and Dom had arrived, they were with Mike Dipalma and John Lucido, two more of their good friends. The four went up to the casket, but only Dom knelt on the kneeler in front of the body and made the sign of the cross. He didn't say a prayer. He would have recited the "Our Father" without listening to the words, but his mind raced over the proper protocol for a wake. He didn't want to do anything wrong.

It was a thankless job attending funerals. There were certain expectations about how you should act and how much money you should leave the grieving family in an envelope. If you were wealthy, though, or free with your money, you would be appreciated, but almost everyone who simply did what was expected was just recognized for it and received the same store-bought thank you letter. You were never appreciated but instead treated similarly when a death occurred in your family. So the focus of the grieving family was often on what anyone might do wrong. There was always a scandal at every function so Dom was careful about his actions. He didn't want to become the next victim of malicious scrutiny.

Alongside the coffin, Stumpy and the others stood behind Dom and stared down at what once was Peppi Bardutti. Everything about the corpse was perfect. There were no wrinkles in the eyelids, nor any shriveling of the skin, not even a hair was out of place. There was nothing dead about the exterior of the body. Inside, though, they could only imagine the scarred and swollen heart that had failed Peppi. The heart condition was called myocarditis, and in Peppi Bardutti's case it was brought on by a rare viral infection: adenovirus type 2. Of course, no one from town believed the virus had caused Peppi's death. Everyone knew that Peppi Bardutti and his bunch were into drugs. Everyone was sure it was speed or coke that killed him. Even the people who believed he had contracted the rare virus were sure it was brought on by drug abuse. It couldn't just be random. But it was.

When Dom rose and moved away from the casket, the others followed and they went up to Peppi's father, who stood to the left of the casket. Mr. Bardutti had composed himself for the moment and wouldn't cry again until Peter Perazzo, the mortician, would ask everyone to leave at nine. One by one the boys shook his hand and said how sorry they were. Stumpy just patted him on the shoulder and didn't bother to reiterate what was said three times over in less than 15 seconds. The old man looked pretty bad, they noticed, like he hadn't slept for several days. He looked completely broken and more prepared for death than the corpse that was laid a few feet from him.

Mrs. Martin, Peppi's mother, sat on the couch that faced the casket. There were rows of chairs behind her, with the closest relatives in the first few seats. Mrs. Martin's sister was on her left and her two daughters were on her right. Her current husband, Bobby Martin, remained in the back, yielding to Peppi's biological father.

Stumpy sneaked past Mrs. Martin, hiding behind his friends so he wouldn't have to say anything. He walked past five of Peppi's closest friends, who were lined up like soldiers on the left of Mr. Bardutti. Stumpy only nodded to Jimmy Baker, the leader of the group, and then he moved to the back to bullshit with those who hadn't been as close to Peppi and with some who had barely known him.

In the back, Dominic scolded Stumpy for not offering his condolences to Mrs. Martin.

"She's too far gone," Stumpy explained. "What could I do to help? I'd only be botherin' her. She looks like she wants to be left alone."

"Don't make excuses. You shoulda went up to her."

"She's not gonna remember. I don't even think she knows who's here."

"You shoulda gone. It woulda helped. Parents remember stuff like that."

"You're full of shit. You don't know that."

"You just don't care."

"It's not my fault he died."

"You don't know nothin'."

"Look, Dom, you live by your rules, I'll live by mine. I care about things. They're just not the same things you care about."

Dom wanted to tell Stumpy more about the way things are, but Mr. Bardutti made his way towards them so Dom just straightened up and remained quiet until the old man passed and went down the stairs that led to the back room where the coffee was served. The boys moved further back and sat in the far room where the chairs no longer faced the coffin. They could talk more freely there and not have to worry about disturbing the mourners.

Clara Puckett was there along with her retarded brother, Lenny. Clara was known as one of the town's sluts, but she was also the part-time girlfriend of Jimmy Baker, the leader of the group that Peppi Bardutti had roamed with. Clara was treated with respect when she was with Jimmy Baker, and like a slut when she wasn't. If she had come alone she would have stood up front next to Jimmy, or perhaps behind him, but she was with Lenny and forced to remain in back where she'd be subjected to ridicule. You couldn't show proper respect with your retard brother along.

Mike Dipalma blurted to Lenny, "How's it going, tard?"

Dom got up and walked away. He didn't have to defend a retarded kid. It wasn't in the town's unwritten code of honor. But Stumpy told Mike to shut up. He was sitting next to Clara, and Lenny was on the other side of her. Everyone except Clara knew why Stumpy defended the tard. Clara was alone and so free game. She was a slut.

ಐ **Ⅽℛ** ℭ **ℰ౦** ℭℛ

Stumpy was thinking of Clara's round, young ass, when Dom finished dressing and put a white rose into his lapel. "You ready, Stumpy?"

"What?"

"You ready to go? The suit's fine."

"Oh . . . yeah."

"You alright, Stump?"

"Yeah. I was just thinkin'."

"About what?"

"Peppi Bardutti's wake."

"Yeah?"

"I was thinking about Clara Puckett."

"She's got a great ass, huh?"

"Yeahhh."

"Well, let's get goin'. We gotta pick up Mike and John."

"I'm ready. You drivin'?"

"Have to. No one else could get a car."

They left Dom's bedroom and Mr. and Mrs. Direnzo were getting ready in the room down the hall. Dom's parents were older than Stumpy's, in their sixties, and Stumpy rushed through the hall and down the stairs without looking back. He didn't want to see the vulgar reality of aging. He had seen Mrs. Direnzo's flabby thighs from behind once and was grossed out by the varicose veins, liver spots and patchy complexion. Dom shouted to his mother that he'd see her at the wedding.

"Take the Regal," she shouted back.

"Yeah, yeah, yeah," Dom muttered. He already knew. His parents never let him take the Oldsmobile, unless it was an emergency and the only car available, and even then, if one of his parents were around they would drive Dom before letting him take the Olds.

Outside, the boys piled into the 1976 Buick Regal. It was a gaudy model, maroon in color, and looked ten years old even though the Direnzo family bought it new less than three years ago. Dom was responsible for the two dents in the front panel and most of the nicks, but his parents had given up on the car too and hadn't bothered to clean it or care for the engine after the first dent.

Dom whipped out of the driveway backwards, screeching the tires, and then he popped the transmission into drive and buried the accelerator. He drove along Birch Street the way most kids in town drove, speeding along and only slowing at the stop signs before rolling through the intersections. Their heads rocked back and forth along the way. The reckless style of driving had claimed many family pets' lives and some squirrels and birds, too. Certain kids around town even made a game out of running down animals and awarded points when you brought the carcasses to the softball field in Patriots' Park. You'd get a hundred points if you hit a bird or a cat. There were always more points awarded for the faster and less amiable animals. The person with the most points at the end of the month won a case of beer.

When Dom pulled over at the Dipalma's house, he gave three long blasts on the horn and looked out the window for Mike. Mike didn't show immediately.

"Let's get John first," Stumpy suggested. "I don't wanna wait."

"We can wait a minute."

"You know Mike. He's never ready."

"Yeah . . . maybe you're right."

Dom drove on straight for seven more blocks and then he turned left onto Fifteenth Street.

"Hey, there's that tard, Lenny," Stumpy said.

"Where?"

7

"Walking on the sidewalk."

"Is he going to the wedding?" Dom asked.

"Of course he's going. He's Clara's brother."

"Half-brother."

"So?"

"Well, what if he does something stupid? He's a tard."

"What's he gonna do, Dom?"

"I don't know. They caught him masturbating in the sauna at the Racquet Ball Club."

"Who caught him?"

"I don't know. Someone did."

"Who told you?"

"Everyone knows. It's all around town."

"Everybody knows, but no one knows who caught him."

"I didn't ask."

"I don't believe it. Why would he masturbate there? Why wouldn't he just go home?"

"He's a tard."

"I guess. Are you sure he did it?"

"Ask anyone," Dom dared. "Everyone knows."

"I believe ya. I don't have to ask."

Dom pulled over when he came to John's house, really John's mother's place, and he blasted the horn again. John didn't show immediately either but there was no one else to pick up, so they waited. It was quiet in the car for a moment but then Stumpy got anxious and talked about what was in his head.

"I can't believe Jimmy's gonna marry Clara."

"Why?" Dom asked.

"Would you marry someone if you knew they'd slept with one of your friends?"

"I don't know."

"Would you marry Clara?" Stumpy persisted.

"Of course not. Would you ever sleep with Marissa?"

"She's your girlfriend, Dom. I'd kick her ass if she came on to me."

"Then I don't have to worry."

"I don't think you do. Marissa doesn't even fuck you."

Dom got angry. "Should I go out with a slut?" he snapped.

"I didn't say that. I think you're doin' the right thing."

"Sure you do," Dom said.

"Well, how come she's not coming with us?"

"Who?"

"Marissa."

"She's got some christening to go to. Her cousin's kid."

"Her cousin? How old is she?"

"Same age."

"Same age?! Scare . . . ry."

"What?"

"She's the same age and married already."

"Just shut up. I ain't gettin' married."

Stumpy laughed and Dom stared at him but it didn't stop the laughter.

"Hey, there's John," Stumpy said. "Now we can get Mike and get out of here. I wanna get this wedding over with."

"No shit. You think I wanna go to this stupid thing?"

"I don't think anyone does."

ༀ ༀ ༀ ༀ ༀ

Almost two hundred people showed for the reception. It was big by some standards but there would have been four hundred or more guests if the parents of the bride and groom were more highly respected.

Jimmy and Clara were leaving the entrance to the hall so they could be announced in as Mr. and Mrs. Jimmy and Clara Baker, when the four boys arrived. They each had their own envelope that they handed over to Clara. The envelopes contained the same amount of money, a hundred dollars, which they all agreed was the proper amount. They always gave twice the amount their plates would cost: an amount they usually knew to the penny because Dom's mother always called the hall and coaxed the plate price out of the banquet coordinator.

One by one they kissed the bride, who trotted off afterwards to hand the envelopes to her mother who had taken her seat at the first table. Then the boys went over to shake Jimmy's hand. Jimmy didn't want to see them, nor any of the kids his age from Rosewood. He was embarrassed about getting married. Like marriage could only happen to someone who had given in to a weakness. He shook hands reluctantly one by one and just turned away when Stumpy reached out.

Stumpy patted him on the back and said, "Don't worry, Jimmy, we don't think any less of you 'cuz you're whipped."

Jimmy turned, his face tightened by anger. "Fuck you," he growled.

"Take it easy," Stumpy said, stepping back. "It was just a joke."

"You're nothing but a coward, Frank."

Dom moved up behind Stumpy and nudged him forward, but Stumpy rolled away.

"What's with him? It's his wedding," Stumpy said, walking off. He went over to their assigned table and sat.

Dom stared at Jimmy and waited for him to say something else, but when he didn't, Dom didn't know what to do.

Jimmy shrugged.

"Let's go to the bar," Mike suggested from behind. "Before it closes."

Dom nodded and they left without saying anything else to Jimmy.

They walked over to the bar and didn't see anyone behind it until they got there and then they saw a man bent over counting the inventory of empty bottles on the floor. They stood quietly a few moments before the man finally lifted his head only long enough to say that the bar was closed until after dinner. Mike pulled out a double-sawbuck and he coaxed Dom to do the same. He didn't bother to ask John for money because he didn't expect him to have any extra. He leaned over and dropped the two bills on the floor where the man was looking. The man grabbed them immediately and shoved them into his pants pocket.

"Just one," he said, standing up. "And you have to take them to your tables. You can't stand around the bar."

"Make us three double gin and tonics," Mike told him.

"What about Stumpy?" Dom asked.

"Make it four, and easy on the tonic. You don't even have to put any in."

The man filled four collins glasses nearly to the rim with Gordon's gin and then he splashed a bit of tonic on top from a gun.

"No limes?" Mike asked.

"I put them away," the man explained.

"Let's just go," Dom said.

"But I want limes."

The man opened the cooler behind him and grabbed a handful of limes. He plopped them onto the bar, which was sticky because it hadn't been wiped yet.

Mike looked at Dom. "We paid twenty bucks. We oughta get limes."

"You're right."

"I know I am."

Mike tossed a lime into everyone's glass, two into his, and then they left for the table.

Four of Jimmy's distant cousins were already seated at the same table, two girls and two boys. Stumpy sat in the chair opposite to them and he glared over but no one stared back. The cousins were younger, the oldest was just fourteen.

After Dom, Mike and John sat, there were two free seats with a chair on either side separating the cousins from the

11

boys. No one talked. Neither group wanted the others there. Dom was on Stumpy's left and he handed him a drink.

"What is it?"

"Gin and tonic."

"Thanks."

"Don't worry about it," Dom said, leaning over towards Stumpy to whisper in his ear. "Why didn't you do something before?" he asked.

"Do what?" Stumpy asked in a normal tone.

"He called you a coward," Mike said from the other side.

"I heard."

"Well, what are you gonna do about it?" Dom asked. "You have to do something."

"I don't even know what he was talking about. Why would he call me a coward? It's stupid. He knows I'm not a coward."

"You still gotta do somethin'," Dom repeated.

"What are you talking about? It's his wedding."

"So," Mike said, "he thinks you're afraid of him."

"I'm not afraid of him."

"It looked that way to me," Mike baited.

Stumpy looked at Dom.

"I know you're not afraid of him."

"I would've decked him right there," Mike said.

Stumpy got pissed because he knew it was true. Mike would have gone after him. He had a temper. They all had tempers, but Jimmy's outburst caught Stumpy so off-guard that he didn't have time to react. He was too busy trying to figure out Jimmy's actions.

Stumpy looked over at John, who hadn't said a word yet. "What do you think?" he asked.

"They're right. You shoulda done something. You didn't even say anything to him."

"I didn't think I should at the wedding," Stumpy explained. "But if you guys think I should, I'll get him after the reception . . . outside. You guys make sure no one jumps in. He's a fat slob. I'll kick his fucking ass."

"Now you're talking," Mike said. "Stumpy's gonna kick some ass."

"He's just doing what he has to," John added. "He can't let him call him a coward."

"Listen to you," Mike said.

"What?"

"Since when do you have an opinion?"

"It's right."

"Whatever," Mike said, and then it went quiet.

One by one the courses came and the boys engulfed them furiously. First was a cream of broccoli soup, which was sure to be talked about the next day. Why wasn't the soup minestrone or pasta fussilli, something more substantial? It was followed by a mixed green salad that contained too much iceberg lettuce and then a chicken marsala entree. There was no pasta served on the side with the chicken which left almost everyone unsatisfied, except for the few people who weren't accustomed to eating pasta with their meal.

Stumpy said nothing throughout the meal, except at the end when he blurted, "I don't even feel like I ate."

Stumpy festered inside. He had no answers and grew more and more angry, like the victim of a long drawn-out war. The assault Jimmy had launched on him became solely a personal attack without any provocation to be remembered. He was ready to attack the fat slob now. He was visualizing it in his mind. He would have to use his speed to ensure a victory. If he did, he knew he would win the fight easily, so it was only a matter of how to get the first punch in because he wouldn't let up after that, not until Jimmy was down and dazed and someone pulled him off. That's when the fight would end, when one of Stumpy's own friends pulled him off. It was considered an act of mercy that way and Stumpy would have reclaimed his honor. They wouldn't fight again. There were no second chances. No one from the losing side ever jumped in either, not even to pull the winner off. They might coax one of the friends from the winning side to show mercy sooner, but they would never break it up themselves. It would be considered a third man in, which would disgrace the entire losing side and further humiliate the loser of the fight. Stumpy had it all figured out by the end of the meal.

There were only two hours of dancing after the coffee was served. It was one of those late-afternoon, early-evening weddings in order to cut costs. Jimmy went around with Clara the whole time. There was the removing of the garter belt and the first dance and then some pictures. It was like the couple was rushing through everything so as not to miss out on any tradition. It was hard for anyone there to imagine that the newlyweds were enjoying themselves. Jimmy looked in pain the whole time. He was dragged from one end of the hall to the other.

When it was over, Stumpy waited anxiously outside for his chance at Jimmy. He made everyone stand behind him. Dom looked over his shoulder. "Just follow my lead," Stumpy told him. "I'll take care of everything."

"What are you gonna do?" Mike asked.

"I'm gonna tell him first. I'm gonna tell him I'm gonna kick his ass for calling me a coward."

"Just deck him," Mike suggested.

"No. I wanna kick his ass fair and square. I want him to know it's coming so he can't make any excuses. I don't want him saying I sucker-punched him."

The crowd grew outside and the four boys kept getting pushed back further and further. Stumpy had to stand on his toes to see the exit. "Where the fuck is he?"

"He has to come out," Mike said.

"There he is," Dom said, "by the door."

Stumpy strained to see over the crowd. "I see him. I see him."

"Wait till he comes clear," Dom added.

"I will. I will."

But Jimmy never did come clear. He and Clara were surrounded by people right up until they ducked into their car. They didn't keep a limousine to take them from the reception, everyone noticed, and Jimmy drove himself and his new bride off in his mother's Bonneville.

Stumpy was hot. He didn't want any delays. He wanted his lost honor recaptured as soon as possible. He would have followed the bride and groom to their honeymoon suite had he known where they were staying.

"Fuck, man!" Stumpy shouted. "I couldn't get near him."

"You'll catch up with him," Dom said. "We'll make sure you get a fair fight."

"You should've decked him when he called you a coward," Mike said.

"Yeah, sure."

"You should've."

"Like you woulda."

"I would've. I wouldn't let no one call me a coward."

"Fuck you, Mike! You think I'm afraid of him! I'll kick your ass, too!"

Mike's eyes opened wide. He clenched his teeth. Dom could see the anger in the intensity of Mike's expression. Dom shoved Stumpy away first. "What's wrong with you guys?" he asked.

Neither answered.

"He'll get him," Dom said to Mike and then to Stumpy. "We gotta stick together. We're friends, you idiots."

Stumpy paused to think, before he sauntered over to Mike. He had his chest stuck out and pressed it against Mike's. "I didn't mean it," he said.

"Just kick his ass for me."

"I will. No one's gonna fuck with us. You know I'm not afraid of him."

15

"Yeah, I know," Mike said and he gave Stumpy a head-butt to rile him up.

"I'll get him, Mike. I promise."

"I know you will."

Stumpy smiled, but it was a fleeting moment of relief. Not to worry was easier said than done when you had lost your honor, which meant at least humiliation and perhaps even exile.

On the drive back to town, Stumpy didn't say a word. Dom drove to Patriots' Park and then around it until everyone realized they had nothing to do. It was only a matter of time before someone suggested the inevitable, Sam's Liquor Store. Dom went in to buy. He was the biggest and looked the oldest, not that it mattered much at Sam's. He came out with two six-packs of Old Style in the cans and two eight-packs of Miller Lite in the seven ounce miniature bottles. Mike made Dom return for a half-pint of peppermint schnapps. He didn't think there was enough beer to get properly drunk. Neither did Stumpy, who was glad when Mike pulled out more cash for the schnapps because he was broke.

Dom drove back to Patriots' Park and pulled over on the street that ran along the back side. There were no lights there like there were at the park's entrance and it wasn't as busy of a street. There were two bacci-ball courts and the boys sat along the wooden edges of one. They all took a can of Old Style, left a six-pack in the back seat and threw the rest of the booze in the trunk in case the cops showed.

Stumpy went into the glove compartment and got a can opener. "Who wants to shotgun one?" he asked. Mike said he would.

"Anyone else?"

No one answered, so Stumpy only grabbed two cans from the back seat. He put one can on the bacci-ball court and punched two triangular holes in the bottom of the other so that he made a hole that looked like a "W," and then he handed the can to Mike upside-down. Mike bent over and put his mouth over the hole and then he stood and tilted his head back, popping the tab and letting the beer soar down his throat. Stumpy was counting, one, two, three, four . . . but Mike was finished before the count of four.

"Pretty good," Stumpy said. "But you gotta open your throat. You can't swallow, it takes too long."

Stumpy punched a "W" hole in the second can and he engulfed his beer the same way. Mike could only count to two for Stumpy.

"That's how you do it," Stumpy boasted. "Dom, do one. See if you can beat two seconds."

"Shut up, stupid. There's a cop coming."

"Where?"

"In the squad, behind you."

Stumpy paused and then walked over to the metal trash can, keeping his back to the squad so he could hide his empty beer can. He dumped the can and then turned and walked back. The policeman slowed and stopped the squad when it was in front of the boys. He opened his door, stuck his head out and peered over the roof. No one knew the cop personally but they knew he was the uncle of Augie Bastianello, a kid on their softball team.

"Come on you guys. You can't hang here," the cop said.

"Where do you expect us to go?" Stumpy asked sarcastically.

"Anywhere," the cop returned. "The woman on the corner called in. She's a pain in my ass. She calls in ten times a day. So you can't stay here. I don't want to keep hearing from her."

"Come on," Dom said, and then he whispered in Stumpy's ear. "I don't want him to take the beer."

"Fine," Stumpy grumbled.

The cop sat back down in the squad and closed the door. He coasted slowly down the street while he watched the boys get into their car through his rear-view mirror.

"Where does he expect us to go?" Stumpy said. "They don't give a shit if we kill ourselves as long as no one's bitching about it."

"He's just doing his job," Dom explained.

"Not tonight," Stumpy snapped. "I'm not in the mood for your lecturing tonight."

"Still pissed cause you're a coward?" Dom joked.

"Not funny, asshole."

Mike laughed. He was buckled over in the back seat. Stumpy was in the back, too, and he stared down at the back of Mike's head. John and Dom were up front. The squad had turned and was out of sight.

"We'll see if you guys laugh when I smash Jimmy's face in."

"Stop, you'll scare me," Mike said.

"Fuck you."

Dom leaned over the front seat. "That's enough, you idiots. Where we goin'?"

"Ask Mike. He's got all the answers."

"Just drive around," Mike said, trying to compose himself. "Maybe we'll see someone."

"Sounds good. There's got to be someone around."

Dom drove off slowly making a right onto Eleventh Street and then another onto Birch where he cruised past the park entrance. The town was quiet. Probably a lot of kids had gone into the city, or out west, to continue the wedding celebration at the newest and biggest clubs. The reception left the boys wanting more. Stumpy opened a beer and Dom reached back for it.

"You want one?" Stumpy asked John.

"No."

"Come on. You never wanna get drunk. Have one."

John shrugged and took the beer when Stumpy offered it. Mike opened his own beer and took steady periodic sips. Stumpy guzzled half of his can and let the rest of the beer warm in his hand before he finished it in a second guzzle.

Dom was driving fast along Birch. Once he had passed the park he didn't expect to see anyone hanging around until he got to Washington's school yard. A lot of kids hung there too but more in the day because there were four basketball courts there, the kind with bent rims and metal nets. Only one net was good enough to have a game on, though. Dom slowed when he approached the school and he drove around the block once. The school yard was deserted. Stumpy didn't see because he was looking around the floor for the half-pint of peppermint schnapps.

"There's that tard," Mike said.

Stumpy poked his head up. "That's all that kid does. He must walk the whole town a thousand times a day."

"Well, he can't drive," Dom said. "He's a tard."

"He's going down Sixteenth," Mike said. "Follow him."

"What for?"

"Come on, hurry. You'll miss him."

Dom made a left down Seventeenth so he could come back up on Sixteenth. Mike kept on him to drive faster. When Dom made the corner off Walton and onto Sixteenth, Lenny was nowhere in sight.

"Hurry up," Mike said. "He's probably on Birch. Get to him before he gets home."

Mike just assumed Lenny was on his way home. They all knew he lived three-quarters of a block south of Birch, on Fifteenth.

When Dom pulled around the corner, Lenny was still on Birch so they drove up behind him. Lenny started to turn down Fifteenth when Mike popped his head out the window and shouted, "Goin' home to beat your meat, tard!"

"Fuck you," Lenny squeaked.

"What did he say?" Mike asked.

"He told you to fuck off," Dom answered.

"Stop the car!" Mike shouted.

Dom kept driving.

"Stop the car!"

"Do it," Stumpy added.

Dom had gone down Fifteenth and was almost at Lenny's house when he finally slowed and stopped.

"Back up. Hurry," Mike said.

Dom did and he stopped just in front of Lenny. Lenny wasn't concerned. He tried to ignore them, as he ignored so much of what went on around him. He had done nothing wrong and there was no reason for him to worry about what the boys were thinking.

Dom opened his door and Mike slammed the seat up onto him and flew out. Stumpy followed.

Walking towards Lenny, Mike asked, "What'd you say to me, tard?"

"I said, 'fuck you,'" Lenny answered, timidly. He wasn't capable of lying and his tone was apologizing while his words answered the question put to him.

Stumpy stopped to pick up a red brick and thought to throw it, but he couldn't because Mike was in the way. Mike went right up to the tard and he stuck his face in Lenny's. Lenny looked down and Mike threw an overhand right, landing his fist across the side of Lenny's face. Lenny was dazed, but he didn't go down. He was humped over, hiding his face with his hands and hoping they would all go away and leave him alone.

Stumpy came up from behind, holding the brick high in the air. "You fucking tard," he yelled. He was filled with anger and he wanted Lenny to look up at him. He moved closer and pressed his hip against Lenny's shoulder. He nudged him. He didn't want to hit the tard with a brick but he wanted to scare him, then he could punch him a couple of times and leave. If he could just put the brick down and whack the tard a few times he knew it would rid him of a lot of anger. "Look at me you stupid tard. I got a message for your new brother-in-law."

"Leave me alone and go away," Lenny whined, never looking up.

"Fucking stupid asshole. I said look at me."

"Leave me alone and go away," Lenny repeated, not looking up. He wasn't listening to them anymore. He couldn't think fast enough to listen and react at the same time, or he would have surely looked up to get them to leave.

"You stupid tard!" Stumpy yelled, and he brought the brick down viciously across the tard's head. Lenny dropped hard like a dead fish. Mike backed off. He had heard the blow and knew it was bad. He had heard Lenny's skull crack and the bone thrashing together. Stumpy was still standing over Lenny and didn't see right away what Mike saw. Mike could see the inside of Lenny's head. He was sure that the tard was dead. There was a piece of Lenny's skull, some two inches across, that was only attached by rapidly coagulating blood and gray matter.

"Let's get out of here," Mike said, looking around to see if any lights were being turned on in the houses. "I think you killed him."

"I didn't hit him that hard."

Mike pointed at the hole in Lenny's head.

"Fuck! What are we gonna do?"

A light went on. It was inside Joey Cassone's father's house. Joey was one of them but they took off for the car anyway. Mike jumped into the front seat with John, and Stumpy dove across their laps, not bothering to pull the seat up to get in back. "Get out of here," Mike and Stumpy said together. "Fast!"

Dom did. He had fled from hundreds of fights and it was nothing new.

"Get out of town," Stumpy said. "We gotta get out of town."

"We'll go to my house," Dom said.

"No, no," Stumpy argued.

"But we can hang in my basement. My parents aren't comin' home. They rented a room for the weekend."

"No! We gotta get out of town."

"No, he's right," Mike said. "It'll look suspicious if we leave town. We'll go to Dom's. We'll say we were there all night."

"You think anyone saw?" Stumpy asked.

"I don't think so," Mike said.

"But what about Joey's father?"

"He wouldn't say anything," Dom said.

"I think we killed him though," Stumpy explained.

"We?" asked Mike. "You hit him with the brick."

"What the fuck's wrong with you, Stumpy?!" Dom asked. "You hit him with a brick?"

"I was pissed."

"Shut up!" Mike shouted. "It doesn't matter. We gotta stick together. None of us knows nothing."

"What if someone saw?" asked John.

"Nobody saw nothing. You hear me?" Mike asked, staring at John.

"As far as I'm concerned, I wasn't even here," John answered.

Mike was satisfied with that.

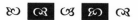

Their story was a simple one and easy to stick to because they had gone straight to Dom's house afterwards. It was only a matter of when they had arrived. They told the cops that after they were kicked out of the park, they went over to Dom's house to play drinking games. There was no one to dispute it.

Almost every kid in town was interviewed as well, some twice and others more. The boys had one of the tightest stories and after the second week they got used to the routine of getting called down to the police station for further questioning. Everyone was being questioned equally and the questions had long stopped being personal. Now the cops were asking them if they saw certain things and they always answered the same, "No, we were at Dom's house." So they didn't think much about being called in a fourth time, especially since the cops wanted to see the four of them together.

When they got to the station they were brought up to the courtroom on the third floor of the municipal building. The mayor was sitting on a bench in the back of the room. The chief of police was up front by the jurors' box and he motioned for the boys to sit there. The two cops who had been questioning them were there but they sat where the lawyers sit, too far to be the ones questioning them now. The front door of the court room was shut and when the chief closed the door behind the judge's bench, it was completely quiet. The boys were nervous now, especially Stumpy.

"Now you're gonna LISTEN!" the chief shouted. His voice rang out and echoed around the room. It shocked them all because they were tense to begin with.

"I don't wanna hear a fucking thing. You hear me?" the chief asked, leaning over towards them.

Everyone shook their heads up and down except for Mike, but Dom nudged him and he shook too.

"I wasn't askin', I was tellin'!" the chief shouted. "You're four fucking knuckleheads."

"But . . ." Mike started.

"Shut-the-fuck-up!" the chief yelled, even louder than before. "I don't wanna know nothing. I already know enough to get my ass in trouble with the fucking state. What do you think we are, a bunch of fuckin' idiots here? You think no one saw you fly down Birch in Dominic's car. You think we don't know who was in town that night. I don't wanna know any more than I already do."

The chief paced back and forth in front of the boys before he spoke again in a quieter tone. "You think I wanna send you to jail for making a vegetable out of some retarded kid? His parents are fucking hillbillies. It was probably incest that fucked the kid up in the first place. He's probably better off now."

The chief paced again. He thought about the problems the investigation had brought him and slowly got angrier. "I've been busting my ass for you knuckleheads. I've been busting my ass trying to convince everyone you were four fucking niggers from Maplewood. That fucking Mrs. Puckett's been in my office everyday for the last two weeks. You boys are lucky no one saw you do it. Otherwise I'd have no fucking choice but to shove your asses in jail. I'm not here to fucking arrest you, I'm here to save my own ass. You're gonna do exactly as I tell you, or we're all gonna wind up in jail."

The chief paced again, letting what he'd said sink in.

"We'll do whatever you say, Mr. Bonglia," Stumpy blurted.

"I told you to listen! Not to talk!" the chief snapped, looking back at all of them, and then he paced more. He paced for almost ten minutes this time and let the boys sweat it out. He wanted to make sure they were listening. They were told to sit there silently and they did, so now he could move on. He gave them a list of things to do in a precise order. It was enough to impress on the boys that the chief had given this routine many times before. First he told them to stick exactly to the story they had given. He said if it was repeated often enough from a lot of different sources, even the soundest of minds would start doubting themselves and their memory. He told them not to tell anyone ever what had happened. He told them it would be attempted murder for all of them now, and murder if the kid died, no matter who hit him with the brick. Yes, they knew it was a brick and they had it too. They would need to destroy it. He let them know how much it was going to cost each one of their fathers and how much it was going to cost John's mother, or John's grandparents, if his mother couldn't come up with the money.

When the chief had said all that he had come to say, the mayor got up and left out the back door without ever saying a word. The chief went out using the door behind the judge's bench and the two officers followed.

The boys didn't know what to make of it. Mike asked, "You think we can go?" But no one answered. They sat quietly for almost twenty-five minutes.

"Maybe Mike was right," Dom said.

"Let's stay a little longer," Stumpy suggested. "We really got away with a big one."

"But he didn't die," Mike said.

"He's a vegetable," said Dom. "He's the same as dead."

"Maybe we shouldn't talk about it," Stumpy suggested.

"We can talk about Lenny," Mike said. "We were at Dom's house when he got beat up."

"You know what I mean, Mike. We really got away with one."

"You got away with one," Dom said.

"You killed a tard," Mike said. "I can't believe you did it. You're a fucking madman."

"You act like you're proud of me."

"I just didn't think you had the balls to do something like that."

"It was an accident."

"What does it feel like?"

"It doesn't feel like nothin'. He's not even dead."

"Sure he is," said Dom.

"Well, if I knew we could've gotten away with it," Stumpy admitted, "I wish I would've smashed that fuckin' Jimmy's skull. I never did nothing to him."

25

The Boteró Woman

U̇RSULA BOTERÓ, KNOWN BY HER CHILDHOOD friends as Lard Ass, looked like an exhibition at a Coney Island freak show sitting on a tiny, three-legged stool. She was a huge woman weighing nearly three-hundred pounds, and although at five-foot-eight she wasn't all fat and had large muscles that gave her an almost square appearance when she stood, when she sat her blubber bulged and melted over the seat of her stool so that if you stood close to her you wouldn't see anything beneath her and she'd appear to be floating somewhere in the center of her drawing room. Even the most experienced person would have needed a moment to get used to her unusual appearance on a stool, but that never occurred to Lard Ass Úrsula Boteró, who cared more about her agenda than her appearance. With such a colossal frame she was concerned about getting even fatter and losing what little mobility she had, so she decided it was best to keep stools around because they took more energy to sit in and she'd be less likely to linger.

Since her early retirement at forty-eight, she had purchased a dozen stools of various heights. She had tall ones alongside the kitchen table, short ones in the drawing room so she could sit and play with her three cats, and medium ones that she hadn't found any use for yet. She had sold or donated every comfortable chair and couch in her drawing room with the exception of an easy chair that she never sat in before ten in the evening. She didn't want the difficulties of getting up to sway her from doing anything she might enjoy and, with a little discipline, she remained remarkably active for a person of her enormity, moving about her four-bedroom apartment for hours on end.

After deciding to bathe, because showers were too difficult for her, Úrsula Boteró's subconscious powers took control and guided her movements. Slowly she spread her tree trunk legs as wide as she could so that her ankle-long dress rose well above her shins. It was not a pretty sight to watch as she dug her hands deep into her fatty thighs, so deep they nearly disappeared, just so she could force her massive self up from that ridiculously tiny stool and lumber towards the master bedroom. With nothing in the forefront of her mind, her subconscious thoughts began to surface and what she had been dwelling on over the last year became clear.

She had been wondering about how to make her life more pleasant and fulfilling now that she no longer had to waste time earning a living. Making it all happen hadn't been as easy as she'd imagined during her thirty years as a manager at Stern's Department Store. She had imagined inviting other cat lovers over for coffee or hosting book discussions on the latest works to appear in the *New York Times Book Review*. There were so many activities she'd thought of hosting, but not one had materialized. The Upper East Side of Manhattan was proving to be far more difficult socially than she'd imagined, much different from her childhood memories of city life that consisted of as many stories her parents nostalgically recalled to her, as memories of her own. But what could she expect? The city wasn't a friendly place, especially looking the way she did.

In her bedroom, standing in front of the full-length, antique mirror that her mother had left her, along with the rent-stabilized apartment, she patiently unbuttoned her pullover dress button by button until the deep crevice, where her navel should have been, was exposed, and then she raised the dress, scrunching it up into a ring until it hung around her neck like a large costume necklace. She didn't just pull the dress over her head like most fat people would have, but instead, bent over, as if attempting to touch her toes, and let it drop to the floor where she kicked it up into her hand and tossed it on the bed. It was an old summer dress that Marta Boteró, Úrsula's rather large mother, had bought in the garment district before she had her stroke at the age of fifty-nine. The dress was dull and worn now but Úrsula Boteró had grown comfortable with it as she had grown comfortable with living alone now that her mother was dead. She had no other living relatives in the States. Her father died two years before her mother and the rest of her relatives were back in Brazil.

With the dress off, Úrsula Boteró slid her bra-straps down off her shoulders and with both hands she dragged the back buckles around to her sternum and unfastened the bra, which recoiled like a slingshot with the loose end whipping around and nearly catching her in the eye. It was a cumbersome, uncomfortable bra with enough wire and fabric to restrain a small child and she truly hated it. Her panties, which could have served as Bermuda shorts for an average size man, bothered her less and she removed them last, as always, and tossed them beside the dress.

She took a step back away from the mirror and examined her nude reflection. Her face was flushed and almost as pink as the nose on her youngest cat when it was excited, and she smiled, noticing herself for the first time in many days. Her long brown hair was falling out of the bun she had tied and she broke a sweat, but for the most part she didn't think she looked that bad. She turned to her side and looked at the body she had long since become comfortable with, forgetting about her childhood days when she never believed she'd accept looking the way she did. She never found men as attractive as her friends did and was happy to be in her body now that she was nearing fifty.

"Women's bodies age much better than men's," she said to herself, "it must be all the added curves." Úrsula Boteró thought of her body as a virtual wonderland with the large waves of flesh flowing and overlapping at the hips and bosoms, and it was at that moment when she decided never to wear clothes again.

The enormous decision seemed plain and sound to her and she began immediately to plan its implementation. All during her bath she tried to think of her daily needs and how she might fulfill them in the nude. By the time she was through bathing, she was so excited to commence with her plans that she phoned the grocer for a delivery even though she had no particular need for anything. All her life she had lived modestly, affording herself only simple luxuries, like the purchase of a new paperback when she couldn't find the used version in any of the neighborhood book stores, but she was meticulous about her housekeeping and rarely needed any household item before she had restocked. She had simple tastes but always kept around her essentials like plenty of white wine and sweets and several kinds of gourmet coffees.

She didn't place a large order with the grocer, but it wasn't small. She didn't want the delivery boy to go out of his way for a few items and she took care to open every cupboard, as well as the refrigerator and freezer, looking for anything that might be running low. After making a list and checking it over, she placed the order, making sure to ask for the total so she could prepare a check. She figured the groceries would fill three bags, and she made sure she had six dollars, two for each bag, so the delivery boy wouldn't have to wait for the check to clear to get his tip. She had an account with the local grocer and knew he accepted her checks. All that remained to do was phone the doorman and let him know she was expecting a delivery, after which, feeling prepared, she returned to the drawing room with the new book she had purchased, *Strange Ceremonies*. She had read the latest review of the book and was excited to read it because the author was an outcast, somewhat like herself, with a self-destructive personality that put her in the most amusing situations. Úrsula Boteró found it absolutely necessary to incorporate humor in any serious work, no matter how horrific the subject matter. "If you can't laugh at life," she'd say, "you'll never make it through it."

Time always went fast for Úrsula Boteró when she read, and the delivery boy had to ring twice before she emerged from *Strange Ceremonies*.

"Oh, that must be the groceries," she blurted and forced herself up from the tiny stool. "How wonderful," she exclaimed, "my first function in the nude!"

She grabbed the money off the end table and lumbered out of the drawing room, down the hallway and into the foyer. The foyer was large for an apartment, square with a high ceiling and a flimsy light fixture, and she didn't look so large standing beside the door. She unlocked the top bolt, then the bottom one and paused before opening the lock on the knob. Quickly she planned in her head what she would say, anticipating the delivery boy's responses, and then she twisted the knob and flung the door open. She stood in the threshold completely nude with an aura of confidence that was usually only reserved for generals in the military, and she waited for the delivery boy to react. She watched him step back and gave him a moment to compose himself.

The delivery boy's face tightened and he scrunched up his nose. "You're fucking nude, ya PIG!" he shouted, with all the malice he could muster. "Look at yourself, you're disgustin'! What's a matta wit' you?!"

Úrsula Boteró's mind raced, and everything she had planned to say was gone when she blurted, "Please understand, I have terrible allergies. I'm not supposed to wear clothes, unless it's absolutely necessary."

"I don't give a shit."

"But I could die!"

"I don't care. Look at you. Are ya crazy or somethin'?"

"Oh, no. I'm not crazy. I would never . . ."

"Ya look crazy to me."

"But if you could just let me have my groceries. I have a handsome tip for you. If you'd just please let me take my things," she pleaded, extending the payment as far away from her body as she could.

"Just put it on the floor," the boy ordered, stepping back with the two bags of groceries in his arms.

Úrsula Boteró did, making the difficult effort to squat and release the payment just inches from the floor so it wouldn't stray, after which she straightened up and asked timidly, "Now could I just have my groceries, please?"

"Yeah, here," the boy snapped, lunging forward and shoving the groceries and Úrsula forcefully so that she lost her balance and went tumbling backwards. "You can choke on 'em," he said, laughing, as she hit the hardwood floor with a crash that was followed by hundreds of smaller crashes of the groceries splattering and bouncing everywhere in the foyer and along the hallway.

"And don't think I'm coming back here," the boy shouted, reaching inside the apartment just far enough to pick up the money and grab the doorknob so he could end the ordeal.

"You'd better find another store!" was the last thing Úrsula Boteró heard before the door slammed with an empathic bang. She was left alone in an awful shock and remained lying flat on her back, staring at the ceiling. She had no perception of time passing and remained still for over thirty minutes, and it wasn't until Gabriella, her oldest and largest

34

cat, approached and sniffed her face that she regained full consciousness. She lay for several more minutes with Gabriella by her side. Gently she stroked Gabriella's head and all the time her emotions crept up on her until she began to sob. Only then, after releasing the emotional stress, did the acute physical pain register.

Úrsula Boteró was not a naive person, but she had never anticipated so much opposition so soon, and it was almost enough to make her reconsider her decision and go back to wearing clothes. It was the time spent on the immediate need to relieve the intense pain that allowed her to forge the strength she would need to continue her life in the nude. The pain was so intense that she left the groceries scattered across the floor, even though she kept a meticulously clean apartment and it made her nervous to have it otherwise. Largely this compulsive behavior was due to her mother, whose attempts at rearing her child properly wound up controlling her and leaving an impression on Úrsula Boteró that she could never shake completely, regardless of her countless efforts.

Úrsula Boteró's entire right side was bruised with one enormous bruise, in the shape of the African continent, that covered her thigh and gave her the appearance of a tattooed sailor. It took her over an hour to tend to her bruises, cuts and floor-burns, and another two to get the apartment back in order. To her surprise, just as she was patching up the last of the groceries, a torn sack of sugar, the doorbell rang. She was not expecting anyone and, for the moment, stood frozen. It was a sharp twinge running along her side that finally stirred her into action and with a fleeting moment of anger, which was a watered-down version of what most would consider anger, she mustered the confidence and determination to answer the door. Being a prudent city dweller, she peered through the peephole first because the doorman hadn't phoned to ask if she was expecting anyone, but when she saw a young man wearing the familiar red and white smock from the grocery store, she was satisfied. She unlocked the door without hesitation and threw it open with the same boldness as before.

"Yes?" she asked firmly.

The young man's eyes widened, and he stood frozen in the doorway. He had to search the annals of his brain for a way to handle this unique situation. The young man had known there was a chance that Úrsula Boteró would be nude when he arrived, but he had deluded himself that either she'd be dressed by then or that he'd be able to conduct himself the way he did in other uncomfortable situations: by ignoring any peculiarities and compensating with an exaggerated sense of ease. He looked directly into Úrsula Boteró's eyes, glancing sporadically up at the light fixture to avoid staring, in a failing attempt to avoid noticing her inevitable nudity, but he drew more attention to his awkwardness than if he had just admitted his discomfort. He made such an effort not to look below eye-level that he didn't even notice the bruises and bandages covering Úrsula's entire right side. Still, she perceived his actions as a conscientious effort not to offend her and warmed her tone.

"What can I do for you?" she asked.

"Mrs. Boteró?"

"Miss Boteró, yes."

"Miss Boteró, I'm Mark du Bois. I'm the personnel manager at Carfour Grocery."

"Yes. I'll understand if you don't want to deliver groceries here anymore."

"No! Not at all. You're a valued customer at Carfour, and have been long before I ever worked there. I've come to apologize for our delivery boy's behavior. I want you to know, I fired him as soon as I heard him telling the story to one of our tellers. What he did was totally uncalled for."

Úrsula Boteró clasped her hands together and rested them over her navel. "Well, he shouldn't have shoved me. But he was just a boy. I probably frightened him."

"Still, it was a stupid thing to do. And it's not the first time we've had trouble with him. I want you to know he won't be causing you any more trouble."

"If you wish to fire him, it's your own business."

"We'd also like to compensate you in some way."

"That won't be necessary."

"We feel it is. We'd like to work out some sort of financial compensation, perhaps a month of free groceries."

"Like I said, it's not necessary. I don't plan on suing. You don't have to worry about that. It's difficult to sue when you don't wear any clothes. You see, I'm not supposed to wear clothes anymore. I've developed a rare condition. My liver produces too much sugar and I run a very high temperature. If I wear clothing, my body temperature could peak too high and I could fall into a coma."

The manager paused, not knowing what to say. He was confused by this large woman's explanation and its differences from what the delivery boy had said. Úrsula noticed his hesitation and waited patiently for him to respond.

"I'm sorry to hear that," he finally muttered.

Úrsula smiled, appreciating his tact and said, "Thank you."

"Still, there must be some way we can compensate you."

"No. That won't be necessary."

"If you're absolutely sure."

"I'm sure."

"Then I'd like you to know, you can continue to receive deliveries at your apartment. I can assure you, you'll be treated with the utmost respect. I'm going to personally have a talk with the entire delivery staff. Or if you'd like, I can even send one of our tellers, if you'd prefer a woman to deliver your groceries."

"Would you?"

"Certainly."

"No, I mean would YOU deliver my groceries?" she said, pointing at the manager.

"Me?"

"Yes. You seem like a nice man."

"Well, it's not the usual practice that I leave the store."

"You said you'd like to compensate me for my trouble. It would make me feel much better knowing you'd be delivering my groceries."

"Oh . . . I wasn't refusing. Of course I'll do it. I was just saying that it's unusual. But you're less than a block from the store. I don't think it would be much trouble. I could even deliver them at the end of my shift, on my way home."

"I'd feel much better if you did."

"Then it's settled. I'd be glad to. And again, I'm very sorry for what happened. There's no excuse for it."

"Well, thank you for stopping by, Mark. Mark du Bois, isn't it?"

"Yes," he answered, fumbling for his wallet to retrieve a business card. "You can ask for me whenever you want a delivery."

"Thank you, I will."

"Have a nice day."

"You too, Mark," she shouted, watching him walk down the hall. When he stepped into the elevator, Úrsula Boteró closed the door and fluttered about the apartment with the giddy excitement of a teenager who had just discovered love. Partly she was infatuated with the idea of making new friends and partly she felt triumphant. She went in and out of the kitchen twice before she remembered the book she had left, and then she returned to the drawing room and sat back down on her reading stool. She sat a moment with the book in her lap and then got up and returned to the kitchen because she knew she wouldn't be able to read unless she had something warm in her stomach, like a hot chocolate. When she returned to the drawing room, she took comfort in the late hour and settled into her easy chair. She read the entire novel, which took over two hours, and then turned in for the night.

ℬ ℭ𝔯 𝔠𝔰 ℬ ℭ𝔯

The following morning she woke with a smile and only a vague recollection of her dreams. She had dreamed she was in the audience at the circus with hundreds of skinny people, without asses, fluttering around her in a flurry of excitement. It left her with a perturbed but happy feeling that remained with her throughout her morning ritual of brewing a full pot of coffee that she would reheat in the microwave cup by cup throughout the day. Sitting on a tall stool beside the kitchen table, she read the *New York Times* from cover to cover and then thought about what to do with the rest of the day. It would be difficult, if not impossible, to go out now and she had no desire to entertain any of her former colleagues whose friendships were dwindling, what little friendships there were to begin with. She didn't think any of them would understand her decision to live nude, especially since they never understood even her simpler choices, like deciding to dress modestly even though she worked at a major department store and qualified for a forty percent discount. In fact, she was sure they wouldn't understand because they had been part of the reason she'd made the decision in the first place.

She was left with no other choice but to spend the day alone, so she decided on pampering herself. After reading the paper, she took a long, hot bubble bath, pouring in both oil and perfume. She wanted to make herself more appealing now that she was roaming around in the nude. She painted every nail on her body with a gaudy hot-pink polish, more out of an ignorance of fashion than to make any statement. She never spent more time on her appearance than was necessary to look proper, and she never paid for what she could do herself. When she was finished with her nails, she colored her hair with henna from a home dye kit, completely staining and ruining her nails which she cleaned afterwards and polished a second time. When the dye set, she washed her hair and, like her mother did for her when she was a child, she dried it with a towel and brushed it with over a hundred strokes because twice she had lost count when she floated off into elaborate daydreams. She dreamed about being the next Janis Joplin and a congresswoman, imagining herself doing all this in the nude, of course. For the final touch, she used a curling iron to bend the ends of her hair outward so she could wear her hair down without it tickling her back.

In the evening she prepared herself an elaborate meal. She made arroz con pollo with lots of fresh chopped vegetables and she fried up some plantain bananas as a side dish. She even prepared a small pan of flan for afterward, so she could have something to take with her coffee. She ate formally in the dining room, setting the table complete with silverware, crystal and two white candles. She drank two glasses of white wine with the meal, instead of her usual one, and had a sweet brandy afterwards to help her digest.

During her first full day in the nude, she enjoyed herself thoroughly and didn't even notice she was alone. With the radio on most of the day, there was enough noise not to notice the drudging silence of solitude, but in the following days she began to feel uneasy.

After her decision, she had anticipated facing loneliness and had planned accordingly. She forged ahead as if her loneliness was only temporary. She mail-ordered for the cheapest computer available so she could chat with people over the Internet, disregarding the advice of the salesperson not to use her real name as a screen-name. Also, her priest began to visit on Tuesday evenings because she was no longer welcome inside the church. Every visit was similar to the first, where Father Vincente urged her to reconsider her decision, but she soon grew tired of the monotony and insisted that he hear her confession first in order to get the conversation flowing and away from her nudity. She began working again, part-time, out of her apartment. She found an ad in the *Times* from a telemarketing agency. She was hired to sell extra services for a local phone company, and they paid her by the amount of orders she mailed in. The work kept her busy and helped to pass the more difficult morning hours.

Everything she tried, in its own way, helped alleviate her loneliness, but nothing removed it. It was a dilemma that, after an entire month of living in the nude, she could find no way out of, never once considering putting her clothes back on, when on the morning of September 18th the intercom phone rang from downstairs and she went to the door to answer it.

The doorman explained that there was a woman from the *New York Times* who wished to see her. Úrsula Boteró found this quite strange and insisted on speaking with the woman.

"This is Úrsula Boteró," she said. "How can I help you?"

"Miss Boteró, you don't know me but we have a mutual friend, Mark du Bois," the woman lied. Really she had overheard Mark du Bois conversing in a local diner and badgered him until he surrendered Úrsula Boteró's name.

"You know Mark?" Úrsula said in a tone that rose along with her excitement. "Oh, he's a sweet one, isn't he?"

"Yes," the woman answered. "We were talking about you yesterday, and I was very intrigued. I was hoping you might agree to an interview for 'The City' section. I understand you subscribe to the *Times*."

"If you're a friend of Mark's. I trust any friend of his. Give the phone to the doorman, and I'll have him let you up."

Úrsula Boteró welcomed the woman simply because she'd mentioned Mark du Bois, but in the time she spent waiting for her to arrive at the front door, she realized the potential positive impact that an article in "The City" section could have on alleviating her loneliness. When the reporter knocked at the door, Úrsula Boteró put on her best face, chased her cats away from the door and then twisted slightly to her side, in an attempt to hide her remaining bruises, before she swung the door open.

"Marvelous," the reporter said, her young, brown eyes opened wide. She was very well dressed and groomed, complete with a new tan overcoat and leather attaché. Her wool pants, protruding from the bottom of her coat, were intricately woven and fresh from the cleaners and her black suede boots lacked the slightest scuff. Nothing she wore looked like it had been worn more than once. From her age, Úrsula guessed it was the woman's first job, and from her attire she assumed she was of wealthy stock.

"Please, come in," Úrsula said, backing up and twisting further until her back rested against the hallway wall and she faced the drawing room.

The reported entered and moved towards Úrsula until she stood directly in front of her, and then, sensing something awkward, she peered around Úrsula's side to see the faded bruises. "Are you all right?"

"Oh, yes. I'm sorry. You can't hide anything when you're naked."

"If it's a bad time . . ."

"No. No. Not at all. I just had a bad fall awhile ago. But never mind. I'm fine. They're only bruises. Please . . . come into the drawing room," she said, walking around the reporter and into the first room on the left. The reporter followed.

Úrsula Boteró motioned to the easy chair saying, "Please, have a seat."

"No," the reporter insisted, "You take it. A stool will be fine for me."

"Please, that chair's only for guests. I never sit in it. If I did, I'd never get out," Úrsula said, smiling bashfully.

"Oh, I see. Thank you then."

"What would you like to drink?"

"That's not necessary. I don't want to take up too much of your time."

"Don't be silly," Úrsula insisted. "You must have something. I have coffee already brewed, or there's tea . . . or soda."

"A coffee will be fine then, thank you."

"Wonderful," Úrsula said, waddling out of the room only to return with a standing tray that had two cups of coffee, a plate of biscuits and some napkins on top.

"I want to thank you for the opportunity to tell my story," Úrsula said, serving the coffee.

"You don't have to thank me. I think it'll make a great story."

"It's such an honor, though, to be featured in the *Times*. I'm so excited."

"Well, you're an intriguing person," the reported admitted, reaching into her attaché for a notepad and miniature tape recorder. "I hope you don't mind if I tape the interview."

"No. Not at all."

"I wouldn't want to misquote you . . . Now tell me, when did you first take your clothes off . . . for good that is?"

"Please, have some coffee first. There's no need to rush. I don't even know your name."

"Oh, I'm sorry. Sarah Parker," she said, placing her pen in her mouth so she could offer her hand.

Úrsula shook her hand politely and said, "Now drink some coffee, Sarah."

She did, taking a quick sip, and then she looked back up, waiting for her host to speak.

Úrsula didn't speak immediately. She carried a short stool over to the tray and, with Sarah Parker watching her like a kid at the zoo, she squatted slowly, lowering herself until she dropped onto the stool, making her flesh and blubber wiggle up and down like warm gelatin. When her body finally settled

43

after half a minute of reverberating, she said, "Well now, let's see. The first time I took my clothes off was in the late sixties. I was very much into streaking back then."

"You've been nude for that long?!" Sarah shouted, straightening up in the chair. "That's incredible!"

Úrsula Botero's face brightened with pride and she thought about not correcting the reporter, when she blurted, "Oh, no, I've only recently been nude for good . . . since my early retirement, over a year ago."

"Well, that's still a long time to go without clothes. Is it a record?"

"I wouldn't know. I'm not doing it for that."

"Then why? It's such an unusual thing to do."

"Unusual, maybe, but I think it was a wise decision for me, if you consider everything."

"And the reason?"

"Well, it's complicated, but I guess I'd have to say I'm doing this for all women. I don't need to tell you what women have gone through over the years for equality, and there's still a lot to be done."

"I'm sure your intentions are noble, but how do you feel living in the nude will help?"

"You certainly are quick with the questions," Úrsula noticed.

"I hope that doesn't offend you."

"Oh, no. This is an interview. You're supposed to ask questions."

"Good . . . Now again, how do you feel this will help women's rights?"

"It's a protest, like any other protest. I expect it to draw attention to the situation."

"Yes."

"Well, I spent thirty years working in a department store, and there were men there with half the time I had, who were making the same salary, more even in some cases. I was constantly overlooked for promotions because I was a woman, that and my appearance. I'm doing this as a protest for all women, especially those whose appearances don't meet up with society's approval . . . as if that matters any."

"Which department store?"

"I'd rather keep them anonymous. I don't really blame them as much as I blame society."

"It would help in getting the story published. I can't promise you it'll make the paper without all the details."

"If it doesn't make it, it doesn't make it. I don't want to bring the store into this. There's no reason to give them bad publicity when they were only doing what everyone else was. There are fundamental changes that need to be made in our society. I don't want to point the finger at anyone in particular. I just want to raise peoples' awareness."

"If you insist. But I can't make any promises."

"I don't expect you to."

"Then let's talk about your daily life. How do you manage? Do you ever leave the apartment?"

"I haven't since I've been in the nude. But I manage quite well. I do a lot by mail, and the custodian helps me with other things. I have my groceries delivered. A neighbor helps me out sometimes, he'll pick things up for me every now and then. It's quite manageable . . . Except for my social life, that's been in an awful mess. I get lonely at times, since I made the decision. Maybe you can help me with that. You know, with the article. I'm looking to host some book discussions, but I need to have people who won't mind my being nude. It doesn't seem to bother you."

"Well, I'm a reporter."

"But surely there are others who can look past my appearance."

"I'm sure there are."

"Perhaps in the article, you can encourage people who'd be interested in a book discussion group to look me up. My number's listed."

"It'll all be part of the story."

"Do you promise?"

"Sure."

"Thank you. Thank you so much. I have to admit when I first invited you up I was a little nervous about giving an interview, but I'm not anymore. I think it'll be the beginning of something really great."

"Good. Then we both can benefit from it."

"Yes, we both can."

Sarah Parker only asked a few more questions before she handed Úrsula Boteró a questionnaire with a return envelope so she would have all the personal details she might need for an article, then she thanked Úrsula and left, not giving any indication when the article might, if at all, appear in the paper.

Sarah Parker wrote an article that not only appeared in the paper, it made the following Sunday paper, portraying Úrsula Boteró as an exciting and eccentric storyteller, more because that story sold papers than because it was the true impression of the writer, but it pleased Úrsula Boteró more than she'd anticipated. There were some things she liked about the article and others she didn't. Stern's Department Store was mentioned for one, but the article was extremely flattering overall and didn't mention anything about the department store's alleged unfair business practices.

The article opened with:

In many ways, as a lifelong New Yorker, there is nothing unusual about Úrsula Boteró, who has spent her entire forty-eight years living on the Upper East Side. Her parents emigrated from Brazil when she was two and she was brought up speaking both Portuguese and English, neither of which she speaks with any noticeable accent. She grew up loving the theater and took a fancy to playing the guitar, which she still plays fairly well, but her biggest passion was and always will be, according to her, literature. The floor-to-ceiling bookcases along all four walls of her drawing room are filled with books and there are still more books piled on the floor, most of which Úrsula Boteró says she purchased secondhand as her salary as a manager at Stern's Department Store afforded her a comfortable but modest lifestyle. She is friendly and outgoing and still adheres to a formal protocol whenever she receives guests. Dropping in on her, she insists that a visitor have something to drink, and she serves biscuits before she allows any formal conversation to begin. She has strong opinions on social issues, especially women's issues, and her opinions on literature are accurate and sophisticated enough to read in the 'Book Review.' Úrsula Boteró even admits that she wrote some of her own stories and was known, on more than one occasion, to tell stories to an audience. All perfectly normal for a woman who grew up on the Upper East Side, one might say, but then what is it that makes Úrsula Boteró so unique? Well, it's the fact that she does all this, at least for the last year, in the nude. Yes, I said, in the nude. Úrsula Boteró has spent the entire last year without ever putting on a single article of clothing.

The article went on for two more columns and there was even a smaller, follow-up article that appeared the following week on the effects Úrsula Boteró might have on the full-figured women's fashion industry. Both articles received a tremendous amount of enthusiasm, so much so that within two weeks Úrsula Boteró had so many parties scheduled that she began refusing people. Within days she felt compelled to make a set of rules for when to turn people away. Her first rule was never to allow more than eight people over at one time because she didn't think she could properly entertain more than that, but that rule was broken before her first party came together when two big names, an editor from Farrar, Straus and Giroux and another from *The New Yorker*, wanted to meet her. She was so thrilled to have people with such prestigious positions wanting to meet her that she insisted they come to her first party, which she had strategically planned to fall on the Sunday before Columbus Day so more people would be likely to show on the day before a holiday.

Everyone was given more than a week to free their schedules, and on the day of the party, Úrsula placed an order from the grocer for things she wouldn't need that night because she was hoping to persuade Mark du Bois to stay when he arrived with her order. The rest of Sunday she spent preparing: arranging cheese and fruit platters, filling specially-cupped biscuits with caviar and stocking the rolling bar with glassware and liquor. Remembering the proper protocol for a cocktail party, she removed every stool from the drawing room and set up a folding table with folding chairs scattered along the walls. She ushered her three cats into her bedroom, where she had placed their litter box and food, and continued preparing until well into the evening.

The first guests arrived at eight-thirty and Úrsula didn't give them time to feel uncomfortable. Within moments she moved them into the drawing room, served wine and filled their hands with napkins and hors d'oeuvres. The two women were interested in moving their book discussion group to Úrsula's apartment and they had accepted the party invitation as a chance to meet with their prospective host. The older and heavier of the two women was admiring the room. "This room is perfect for a book discussion," she said. "All the books, you're obviously well-read. Just the type of person we're looking for . . ."

"Oh, thank you," Úrsula said, interrupting the woman so she could go answer the door. An avalanche of people began to arrive and within thirty minutes there were more than fifteen people scattered around the drawing room and along the hallways. More than half the guests had brought a friend, and everyone wanted to meet Úrsula Boteró. She was overwhelmed by the attention and the running around trying to serve and socialize at the same time. She met with the two editors, who were very formal and pleasant on the surface but filled with questions. They wanted to know everything from where she went to college to how serious she was about writing.

In the beginning, though, everyone was full of questions, but over the course of the night, most of the guests became less fascinated with Úrsula Boteró and more interested in the free food and liquor. She had gone through six bottles of white wine and three of red, and some of the guests had even wandered into the kitchen to peek inside the refrigerator.

It was a mixed group and not all were bad. Úrsula liked the two women who had arrived first and she hoped they would move their discussion group to her apartment, but there were other guests she didn't like. One woman had brought her boyfriend, a tall, thin, attractive man dressed entirely in black. Úrsula Boteró overheard him saying to his girlfriend, "What are we doing here? The article's a fraud. This woman's no storyteller. She's just a fat, lying pig." It didn't take Úrsula long to realize that this party was no different from any other party she had hosted, except for the obvious: She was nude.

When Mark du Bois arrived with the groceries, a few of the guests were preparing to leave, including the two editors who had arrived together just twenty minutes earlier. Úrsula asked Mark if he could carry the groceries into the kitchen, and he gladly obliged.

Úrsula followed him into the kitchen where she took a seat on one of the tall stools beside the table, and she purposefully didn't pay Mark immediately. One of the guests poked her head in. "Oh, sorry," she said, "I was looking for the bathroom."

"Go back down the hall and make the first left. It's at the end of the hall."

Mark du Bois had a surprised look on his face and when Úrsula didn't speak to him immediately he grew uncomfortable and spoke to break the silence. "It's quite a party," he admitted.

"Yes."

"It's pretty amazing."

"What?"

"That you can throw such a party," he said, pausing and wanting to add "in the nude" because her being nude made no difference to him. In the end he said nothing, though, because he didn't want to draw attention to Úrsula's nudity.

"I don't think it's that amazing," Úrsula answered.

"I do. I'd never have the courage you do."

"Really, it's nothing."

"I still think it's amazing. Who would have ever thought?"

"Thought what?"

"Well . . ."

"Well what, Mark? You don't have to be bashful. Say what's on your mind."

"That you could throw a party . . . in the nude."

"Oh, that," Úrsula said, laughing. "This is my first one in the nude, but you'd be surprised how typical it is. This party's hardly any different from any other one I've hosted."

"It's wild, though."

"It's not that hard."

"But there are so many people."

"Yes, you've got me there. I never expected so many people to take an interest in one nude woman."

"I think it's great."

"So did I, at first. But these people aren't interested in me. They only want to know why I'm naked. Once they've satisfied their curiosity, their interest goes away."

"I'm sorry."

"It's not your fault," she said, pausing a moment before continuing. "But at least you're different. You seem to listen to me, and not let my nudity bother you."

"I guess."

"You know, Mark, I want to tell you something."

"What?"

"I want to tell you the truth about why I stopped wearing clothes."

"Really, Miss Boteró, that's not necessary."

"Please, call me Úrsula. And that's exactly why I want to tell you." She paused to catch her breath and after a minute she straightened herself up on the tall stool, keeping her balance with the tips of her fingers pressed against the table. Her breasts hung low, almost down to her navel, but she held her head up.

"You see," she began, "several weeks ago I was getting undressed to take a bath. I was staring at myself, naked, in the mirror, and it just dawned on me that I might be happier if I only socialized with people who could get past my choice to live nude, especially looking the way I do . . ."

The Passing
of the Reins

W HEN TERESA PUCCINI DIED, HER TEN SONS knew they had to meet in the basement apartment of their deceased parents' home, so they could argue, with a fierce and relentless passion that often became violent if agreements weren't reached quickly enough, over what eventually they would all agree upon was the one and only proper procedure to follow. On their way over they would pick their brains, like vultures at a carcass, for stories of how things had been done in the past. They would recall and embellish deeds their mother had performed in the name of the family, trying to inflict a sense of obligation on each other, a feeling that already thrived. They would callously fling guilt back and forth across the table as if it were a Frisbee, crushing the self-esteem of even the proudest boy, and guilt was only one of the weapons their parents had taught them to wield in order to maintain the family's hierarchy and affinity.

Each boy would come prepared to fight for his notion of how everyone should pay their final respects, yielding only to the pressure of a unanimous disagreement by the remaining brothers. Theirs was a crude and sometimes vicious family government, but it managed to endure, granting individuality solely to the strongest and most worthy family members, who would in turn, with time, influence the family and bridge the gaps between generations, bringing the family closer to its inevitable dismemberment.

It was understood that the heated discussions would begin when the last of the ten boys arrived to take his seat alongside the kitchen table, where the family gathered to do almost everything from dining to playing cards to the more serious matters like planning a relative's wake and funeral, or counting the intake of money from a grand wedding. The table, like many objects around the house, was a permanent fixture in the boys' lives, being there as far back as the eldest could remember, and they thought fondly of it as if it were a photo album, containing in its mere appearance the ability to summon up the most distant memories from their childhood.

There was always a battered tablecloth covering the table so that it was only familiar to them with its checkerboard mask, and it was a disturbing and shocking sight whenever one of the boys remained in the kitchen long enough after dinner to see the unnatural color of the metallic brown Formica whenever their mother removed the tablecloth to wipe down the top. The table had two pullout leaves, one at each end, which was a typical design for a table built in 1954, when Teresa Puccini bought it shortly after giving birth to her third son, Jonathan.

"We're going to need the extra space," Teresa told her husband, Guiseppi, thinking at the time she would bear at least six children, maybe eight, if she were to even out the ratio of boys to girls.

All of the boys entered the house the same way they always did, going through the side door where the staircase led directly to the basement so they wouldn't disturb the main floor, which, even when the house was filled with children, was rarely ever used. Had the boys entered through the front door, they wouldn't have noticed the gradual changes that had transposed their mother's favorite room from a gallery-like drawing room to a neglected attic atmosphere with stale, dead air and scandalous cobwebs.

They wouldn't have noticed how the sun had faded the carpet and upholstery, nor how time had yellowed the plastic covers that were zippered up around every piece of furniture in order to preserve them in the sanctuary of their original form. They wouldn't have noticed how the dust and filth had embedded inside every nook and cranny of the elaborately carved wooden picture frames and both the antique wooden cabinets cluttered with knickknacks that Teresa had acquired over the years on her weekly trips to the city, so that nothing was as brilliant as it had always been when their mother was caring for the house. The main floor hadn't changed at all during the forty years that Teresa had watched over it, but the years of her illness, before her death, had taken a depressing and devastating toll, even though the front room hadn't been used by any of the boys.

Before her husband died, Teresa managed the front room with a diligence and compulsion that brought her much satisfaction. She guarded it with pride, dedicating it for the entertaining of special guests and family members who visited from overseas. It wasn't often that someone was honored to enjoy its ambiance. The last time was eight years before Teresa's death, when Sister Mary Rosetta was invited over for dinner to celebrate the graduation, from St. Jude's grammar school, of Teresa's youngest son, Augusto. Teresa wanted to show her appreciation for all the extra help Sister Mary Rosetta had granted Augusto to get him through the seventh and eighth grades. It was the perfect opportunity for Teresa to reap the profit of years of sacrifice and hard work that she had expended caring for the front room, and indulge herself in her own martyred efforts, a pleasure she had expertly learned, being the mother of ten boys and having to constantly sacrifice for their well-being.

Teresa never knew that Sister Mary Rosetta spent extra time with Auggie out of fondness for him and not out of obligation. Being sent to a new parish every three years by the Catholic Church, Sister Mary Rosetta rarely had the opportunity to make friends, and when she noticed something special in Auggie, she befriended him immediately. Auggie was doing poorly in school, but he wasn't a slow child. His attention wandered more often when he entered junior high. He had always been a maverick, where even if he didn't physically drift away from the other children, his mind was usually far off, and when he started spending less time with the other children and more with Sister Mary Rosetta, she thought of his friendship as a gift from the Lord.

Teresa never thought anything of her son's newfound difficulties with school, brushing them off as the normal havoc associated with puberty. After all, it was the tenth time Teresa had helped one of her sons get over the hurdles of becoming a man. There was even a time when Teresa believed Auggie would make the transition with the greatest ease. Auggie never displayed any signs of having difficulties with puberty, the same signs Teresa had observed with most of her boys. Auggie was nothing like Alfredo, Teresa's second son, who had the sexual appetite of a lion. Her second son also lacked inhibition, just like his father, and he had a strong sense of logic, too, so he never believed the priests at Sunday catechism school when they preached about the sins of allowing masturbation to become a habit. If the Lord could look the other way for Alfredo to masturbate once a week, why couldn't he look the other way once a day, or even more often for that matter? At one point Teresa grew so concerned over Alfredo's enormous appetite that she sought the advice of the family physician. His appetite couldn't be normal, she'd thought. Every pair of Alfredo's underpants were soiled when she went to wash them, and not just in one spot, along with the crusted stains she had found on his socks and undershirts, and both the insides and outsides of his bed sheets. She was doing two loads of whites a week just to keep up with Alfredo's fury. Teresa imagined him as a butter churn worker gone mad. But as time passed and more of her sons braved through puberty, Teresa learned for herself that the doctor was right when he said that not only was it normal for a boy but common.

Teresa only noticed the onset of puberty affect Auggie, when puberty to Auggie was still an unknown source of energy and sensation that came from nowhere in particular and couldn't be channeled off in any given direction, so it was tolerated with a pleasant sense of curiosity and bewilderment. Once she had caught Auggie wrestling with his manhood, sitting on the floor in front of the television in the basement. He could have been wrestling an alligator the way he had a hold of his dick, and she could tell from his ferocity that he wasn't about to release his grip until he had squeezed every bit of life out of his still half-sized monster. Teresa smiled and turned away that day, wondering when Auggie would learn that a gentler hand would assist him better. She never knew for sure if he'd learned to masturbate properly because shortly after the incident in front of the couch, Teresa never again observed Auggie to have any further fascination with himself, and when his grades slumped, she smiled again, imagining the ruckus he must have been causing, chasing the prettier girls around school.

Auggie loved his mother a great deal, despite her occasional misinterpretation of his motives, because they spent so much time together. Still, he was the only one of the ten boys who wouldn't be at the table when Teresa's sons discussed what they should do now that their mother was gone. Of course his picture would be placed in front of his empty chair, the way it had always been done for every family gathering since his untimely death, and he would always be spoken about in the present tense as if he were still alive. In fact, in the family's eyes, the only difference between Auggie and the rest of the boys was that Auggie no longer aged and no longer did anything wrong. Even when Enzo and John, the only two boys still living in the basement apartment, were telephoned about when everyone should meet, they both said that the ten of us, not nine, should be there by six-thirty, shortly after the oldest boy, Umberto, would finish work.

It was Teresa who first insisted on having Auggie's picture placed on the kitchen table in front of his empty chair, when the arrangements for Auggie's funeral and wake were being made, and it didn't take long before the ritual became a habit and tradition with the family. Auggie had always been Teresa's favorite, even before his death, and the other boys accepted it because he was the baby, some twelve years younger than the next oldest, and Teresa's last attempt at having a girl. At the age of forty-six, with menopause creeping upon her, Teresa was reduced to treating her baby like she would have treated a daughter, befriending him and keeping him around the house as much as she could, as she desperately attempted to get him interested in the less grueling domestic chores.

Teresa took Auggie shopping whenever she went into the city to buy knickknacks for the cabinets in the front room, and she tried to spark in him an interest in baking by allowing him to lick the mixing bowls and spoons whenever she made cookies. Auggie was content enough to endure through all his mother's chores and self-indulgences because he truly enjoyed her company, even though he was very different from her and often somewhere far off in his mind. He was glad to be beside her, knowing it meant a great deal to her, and he did it freely because he loved and admired his mother. He admired the versatility of her abilities and was overwhelmed by the volume of her daily accomplishments. She worked perpetually from morning till night, except on Mondays when she took the train into the city to buy things for the house and herself. She would be up before him in the morning, up serving dinner when everyone else was eating, and up after dinner cleaning. Until late in the evening, Auggie never saw his mother sit down longer than it would take to eat a tiny portion of leftovers, or the nine or ten minutes that came between commercials if she were to watch one of the daytime game shows, and even then she only sat on the edge of her seat in the kitchen peeking through the partition in the wall. "Wheel of Fortune" was her favorite, although Auggie never understood why.

Auggie wished he could be as productive as his mother, but being a very skinny boy and not particularly interested in food, nor in his overall outward appearance, let alone the outward appearance of where he lived, he always felt guilty whenever he left his mother's side, allowing himself to be drawn to his natural interests. Since he was old enough to wonder, he had been fascinated by anything mechanical or electrical, and he wanted to know how everything around the house worked, and a simple explanation was never enough. He wanted to see for himself, up close, whenever anything was taken apart. There wasn't a handyman's chore that his father or brothers could do that was too trivial for him to watch. No one could change something as simple as a light bulb without having Auggie peeking underneath their arms. Whenever Auggie's brother Anthony would repaint the house, Auggie would follow him into every room and sit as close as he could, without being in the way, and remain there as quiet as a frightened altar boy during mass, so he could follow his brother's every move no matter how repetitive some of them were. He'd watch his brother repeat the same task a thousand times, each time further convincing himself that he could reproduce the action without ever having tried it. He would watch as Tony covered the mahogany base trim with tape in order to protect it, and then he'd watch him tape the door and window trim. He'd watch his brother paint along the edges, sometimes taking several hours in the larger rooms, before Auggie could watch him bring the new color of the room together with the roller. Auggie always roused when the roller came out because it meant the job would soon be done. He would have sat for months on end, if that's what it would have taken, to see the job completed because it was the accomplishment that drove him.

Auggie was thrilled the one time Tony didn't have enough paint left that was worth saving, because the odd shade of yellow was only suited for the bathroom, and he gave the quarter of a gallon to Auggie to paint the inside of the family tree house, of which Auggie had inherited sole ownership because he was the only one still small enough to fit comfortably inside it. Auggie got lost for three days afterward, the first day painting, repeating every step identically to the way his brother would have done, and the next two sitting in his tree house admiring his work.

Teresa never knew what Auggie was doing up there those three days and she had to keep calling him down whenever it was time to eat or to wash up or to go to bed. She lobbied the entire three days to get him to spend more time in the big house. She didn't know then how capable her son was, nor how fine a painter he was. She was only pleased when he spent the fourth day with her, helping her fry the meat for Sunday's pasta gravy.

The tree house was torn down after Auggie's death. Teresa had learned to hate it, and not because Auggie fell to his death from it one afternoon, but because she had lost her son to that damn tree house long before his death. It was shortly after his graduation from grammar school, after Sister Mary Rosetta was sent to a new parish in Los Angeles, that Auggie started spending more time in his refuge that loomed over the big house.

Even in the big house Auggie became more reserved. He hardly talked to anyone anymore except his mother and usually only to her when they were alone. Whenever she'd set the table for dinner, before anyone else was home, Auggie would sit in his chair, where his mother was never sure if he was watching her or just staring out into space. Every now and then, very abruptly, he would say, "Mama."

"You can speak," his mother always returned sarcastically, continually trying to change Auggie's way, but he had long since learned to ignore her.

"Would you still love me if I married a black woman?"

"What kind of question is that?" Teresa answered.

"Would you?"

"Who are you talking about?"

"No one."

"There's no one at your school who's black. Why would you ask such a question?"

"Would you still love me?"

"You know I've always taught you that color doesn't matter."

"But what if I married a black woman?"

"Well, you shouldn't. You shouldn't marry someone of a different race. It's not good for the children. Your genes don't mix. It's not right."

"That's not true. Lots of people do it."

"Of course it's true. That's why there's so much cancer and disease now-a-days—because of all the interracial marriages. Now I don't want to hear another word about it."

"Then you wouldn't love me."

"I didn't say that."

"But . . ."

"But nothing. I'm your mother, and you'll do as I say. You understand me? You'll do as I say."

"But that's stupid. You're stupid."

"What did you say? What's gotten into you, Auggie? You never used to be like this. You never used to talk like that. What's gotten into you?"

Auggie answered with a defiant look, and his silence only led his mother to speculate. "You think too much," she told him, "that's your problem. Why don't you go watch some television? Relax once in a while. You know your favorite show is on?"

"I hate that show."

"You didn't hate it a month ago."

"I hate it now."

"Why don't you give it another try? I like it."

"No. I hate it. It's stupid."

"That's because your brothers tease you. Go watch Mr. Rogers. I like him. He's a very nice man."

"No, Mama. I don't want to."

Teresa persisted, despite her son's irritation, because she knew he was more mature than the boys his own age and she wanted him to feel understood and comfortable in the company of as many adults as she could find to spend time with him. It didn't matter to her whether they were real or came over the TV waves. She knew her son perceived a tolerance in Mr. Rogers, a tolerance he deserved, and she didn't want peer pressure to deprive it from him. Still, the more she persisted, the more Auggie fought her. He was his mother's child. Their bickering over Mr. Rogers usually ended with Auggie leaving and going to the backyard and up into his damn tree house.

Auggie had stopped watching television during the days and he fidgeted anytime he watched at night with the family. He stopped lying on the floor, in front of the couch where he used to watch from, and he started bringing his chair in from the kitchen and setting it up behind everyone, between the sectional and the couch. At Teresa's request, Guiseppi would coax his son to come sit on the couch beside him, where Auggie used to sit when he was a baby, but Auggie refused, explaining that he was too old to sit with his father and he didn't like it anymore. "You're never too old to sit with your father," Guiseppi explained the first time Auggie refused, but Auggie snapped back with a fierce, "No! I don't want to! I don't like it!" and Guiseppi surrendered, being too old and wound down to argue with such a vigorous defiance. Still, intermittently, Guiseppi would remind his son that the offer stood.

One time Guiseppi looked back to invite Auggie up to the couch and he found him dozing off, so he told Tony, who was also watching "All in the Family" to lift Auggie and bring him over, but Auggie awoke in Tony's arms and started screaming with terror. He screamed so loud that his mother's heart skipped a beat, and every one of the basement windows continued to rattle long after he'd stopped yelling. It shocked Tony so much that he dropped his brother to the floor with a thud. Auggie was petrified and he glared around the room like a cat that had found itself suddenly surrounded by strangers, and he stared deeply into the eyes, one by one, of everyone in the room. He looked up at Tony first, and when Tony looked as confused as he was, he looked at his mother and then his father and then at Enzo and John. He whipped around to look back at his mother when he heard her speak.

". . . wrong, Auggie? Is there something wrong? Are you alright? Talk to me."

He didn't answer but instead looked up at Tony and asked, "What was I doing?"

"Nothing," Tony said, "I was just bringing you to Papa. Did I hurt you?"

"What was I doing? Why did you pick me up?"

"To bring you by Papa, you little idiot. What's wrong with you? Are you crazy or something? You scared the hell out of me, you little weirdo. You're getting weirder all the time."

"Don't say that to your brother," Teresa defended.

"But he is. He's a little weirdo."

"What's wrong, Auggie?" Teresa asked. "Why don't you come sit by me?"

Auggie turned to look at his mother and demanded, "What was I doing?"

"You were sleeping. Did you have a bad dream?"

Auggie didn't answer. He paused and then pushed himself up off the floor. Tony had sat back down, and Auggie walked to the inside stairwell and started up for the third floor, where at the time he was sharing a room with Enzo and Tony. Teresa asked again if he was alright, to which she only got a grunting, "I'm fine. I'm going to bed."

Teresa worried herself sick over Auggie. He had developed a need for privacy, a need that none of his brothers had developed. Growing up with so many people in the house, his brothers could be oblivious to the presence of others whenever they needed. Teresa blamed Auggie's differences on the tree house, because Auggie was the only one who ever had sole possession of it.

It was a bittersweet day for Teresa, during the late summer, when Auggie went down to the basement and came up with a piece of plywood, a tape measure, a hand saw, a pencil and two rusty hinges that he had removed from the old kitchen cabinet doors that his father had replaced over six years ago. Teresa watched from the kitchen window as Auggie worked. Like a miniature carpenter, he moved efficiently and accurately, the same way he had watched his father and brothers work. He measured a length of plywood at two points, drawing a line between them so he wouldn't cut unevenly, and then he made six other small marks for drilling to be done later. With his thin arms, he sawed steadily with full-length strokes. With a sharp-toothed bench saw that Guiseppi kept oiled and hung upside down in the basement to ward off rust, Auggie ripped through the piece of three-quarter-inch birch plywood as if it were cardboard. His mother beamed with pride, all the time wondering if it were a birdhouse or a wagon or something else being crafted. When Auggie finished the rip, he started a crosscut, leaving himself with a perfect thirty-six by fourteen inch rectangle, which he sanded carefully, first with coarse sandpaper and then with a finishing paper.

Auggie placed the piece of wood on the grass and admired how evenly he had cut, before he went back down into the basement and came up with his father's electric drill, dragging the orange extension cord behind him. With speed and precision, he drilled three holes in the top left corner and three holes in the bottom left corner. Teresa had no idea what he was building until she saw him fasten the hinges to the wood. It was then that her heart dropped, and she didn't want to, but she knew she had to look up. For her, it felt like looking into the street after hearing a long screech from a car's tires along with a loud thump and knowing her children were out playing. With ten boys, she always feared losing one of them to a speeding car, and never once dreamed she would lose one to a tree house, two old hinges, a piece of plywood and a boy's ferocious will.

It deflated her when she heard Guiseppi bragging the next day to the neighbors about his son's gift as a master carpenter, because it sealed the fact that she couldn't deny him his tree house, nor the new door he had built for it. He had worked too diligently and honorably to take care of the tree house, and there was no legitimate reason to condemn it.

In the fall, Auggie brought a space heater up to the tree house, but he wasn't able to keep it there. Teresa thought she had scored a victory when her husband agreed that it was a fire hazard and Auggie was forced to bring it down the same day. Still, it was only a minor inconvenience because shortly afterwards Auggie found an old sleeping bag and some extra blankets to keep him warm. With the new door blocking the wind and some old candles saved for really cold days, Auggie was cozy and comfortable, managing to spend most of the fall, before his fatal plunge, tucked away reading his fitness magazines, comic books and fantasy novels. It was like having his own bedroom, only better because no one could barge in on him. There were too many warnings before anyone could disturb him. He would hear the back door open or the gate to the fence creak, and more often than not someone would yell to him before they would climb the ladder of cut two-by-fours nailed to the tree. Even if they did climb the ladder, he could always latch the door with the bolt lock he had screwed into place.

Everything Auggie treasured he brought up to the tree house for safe keeping. No longer would his brothers wear out the batteries in his radio, or wrinkle his magazines, or make fun of the books he read. After a while he had to build shelves out of milk crates and plywood so he could find the space to sit without smashing something, and it didn't help that he was getting larger all the time and would soon be too large to sit inside without his head pressing against the ceiling.

Teresa kept every book and magazine she found up in the tree house after Auggie's death, along with the blankets, candles, marbles, and other small toys, including a scrambled Rubik's Cube. During the wake she gave strict orders that no one was to disturb the tree house until after the funeral, when she could find the time to go up and inspect it. She personally threatened every one of her sons, some more than once, if they happened to be with someone she hadn't threatened yet, with excommunication from the family if anyone was to even go up in the tree house before she did. She had a sick feeling that perhaps Auggie's death wasn't totally an accident and perhaps was linked to the fact that he was getting too big to keep the tree house, and if that were true, it was a fact that Teresa wanted to hide and bury along with the corpse.

She couldn't put out of her mind the way Auggie moped around the house the days before his fall. It became an obsession with her until November 16, 1989, the day after the wake, when she had Enzo bring her a ladder from the garage. Enzo pleaded with his mother to let him retrieve everything from the tree house, but the best he could do was to be allowed to support the ladder. He watched from below as his mother forced an empty cardboard box through the small opening and then went in after it.

The instant Teresa entered the tree house, she sensed an odor that she had first smelled the morning after her wedding, when she'd wiped herself after making love to her husband for the first time. It was the same smell that came from

Alfredo's soiled underpants and sheets. Stuffed in the corner, she spotted the culprit, a crumpled towel that was once white but was now a dull gray with yellow and rust-colored stains. It was one of the first clues that Teresa distorted to convince herself that Auggie's death was entirely accidental. If he was going to kill himself, she told herself, he wouldn't have left that towel there, he would have thrown it away. He wouldn't have left a magazine next to it either, a magazine that she could tell, by the faded colors of the pages and by the permanent folds, had been opened to the same page for a long time. The page displayed an advertisement for Soloflex, an exercise machine, where a man without a shirt was exercising his shoulders and back. There were stains on the page where the magazine had gotten wet many times, probably from a leaky roof, she thought, although she never bothered to smell it to make sure. She closed it to the cover page, having to crease it heavily and place several other magazines on top to get it to stay in place at the bottom of the empty box. Then she called down to Enzo to bring her a plastic garbage bag, the kitchen size, where she placed only the towel inside before tying it off and personally throwing it away in a garbage can in the alley underneath some bags that she had lifted out. She packed the rest of the books, fourteen fantasy novels and countless comic books, and then placed the Rubik's Cube, marbles and other smaller toys on top, before she sealed the box with duct tape.

She carried the box back inside the big house and placed it in the closet in her room, hiding it behind her hung coats and dresses. There she knew it would remain for safe keeping until her death because the boys feared going into their parents' room, partly from ignorance and partly from the overwhelming pressure that the cluster of relics from a time long before they were born brought on. Their mother had also planted a fear in the boys, suggesting that she was hiding dangerous and devastating family secrets in her room that the boys believed would end the family's harmony as they knew it. But in fact, before the box was placed inside the closet, the biggest secret the boys would have discovered in their parents' bedroom was that the family owned some lakeside property in Round Lake, Wisconsin.

Going into their mother's room after her death was the first thing the boys discussed when they gathered at the kitchen table. They knew they had to go through her things, because she had told them herself many times after she'd gotten sick. She had left her important papers in a shoe box in the top drawer. She had left pictures everywhere, each inscribed with the date and names and relationships of everyone appearing. Inside her purses, jewelry chests, music boxes, ceramic knickknacks and any item of importance, were pieces of yellowing loose-leaf paper with the significant historical facts about the object: where she had bought it and who was with her when she did. In the cedar chest, the size of a coffin, there were scented bars of soap on top of the hand-stitched and hand-woven linens, some from two generations back, some that Teresa herself had discovered in the same cedar chest after her mother's death.

The boys went through everything together, except for the box in the back of Teresa's closet that was sealed with duct tape. Written on the box, in permanent black marker, were the orders, "Never open this box. Burn it in the alley after I'm gone. Do this so your mother can rest in peace."

Their mother's words sent a chill down all their spines and only Tony had thought to suggest they look inside first. The cold and hate-filled looks of the other eight boys were enough to tell Tony instantly that a unanimous disagreement had been reached and he yielded immediately. Still, Enzo couldn't keep himself from jabbing Tony by asking if money was more important to him than his own mother. Tony defended himself, explaining that he was only thinking of the mementos that the family might not want to lose, but his plea landed on deaf ears. It was a dangerous time to speak your mind, and Tony kept quiet after he found himself alone. He just followed Umberto, who carried the box, and his other brothers as they walked outside and into the alley.

Being the oldest and seventeen years older than the youngest living brother, Umberto took charge without any resistance. He would take care of the house now and the shoe box with the important papers was entrusted to him. He held on to the deed to the house, because his mother never discussed selling it and so they would keep it.

Outside in the alley, Umberto gave the instructions, telling Enzo to go get some gasoline from the garage and the others to empty a garbage can so he could put the box inside. No one knew what was in the box because all the boxes they found in the room looked the same, but they followed orders blindly.

When the box was in place, Umberto poured so much gasoline on the dried cardboard that when he dropped a match on top, the flames soared higher than the top of the first floor windows and the siding of the house nearly caught fire. No one could get near the garbage can while the box burned and when it was all over the box was reduced to ash and there were carbon stains on the side of the house. After Umberto wiped down the side of the house with a wet rag, he looked up to the sky and told his mother to rest in peace in heaven with Auggie and Papa.

And with that, Teresa's last wish was fulfilled. She wanted her son, Auggie, to remain what she and her husband were destined to become in the family's eyes: martyrs.

ରେ

*A Different
Way of Living*

IN HIS DREAMS HE WAS DEAD AND HIS BODY
had been laid on the plush, cool grass so that it faced the
sky, which was dark blue with patches of clouds drifting
past, making the sky appear touchable among the infinite
blue. The man's body didn't lie in a coffin, nor underground,
but instead in a field with trees off in the distance. Several of
the man's friends had gathered around but something strange
kept the man from being able to look at them, and his friends
couldn't see him trapped inside his body. His friends had
formed a circle and remained quiet for a while and then slowly in pairs, or one by one, they left until the man's wife was
the only one left. The man knew his wife well and he could
tell without looking at her that she was calm and content to
remain nearby, and he knew that if she should leave, she
would return soon and often. It confused him, though, that she
sensed he was nearby without knowing exactly where.

He thought about this for what seemed to him a very long
time and then he grew tired and shut his eyes, trying to sleep.
He allowed his mind to go free and he could hear the silence
whistling inside his head as he became a part of the field. He
felt his body dissolving in the air and in a whirlwind he was
lifted and swirled about, becoming infinite yet remaining one.
Then he heard a shout, "Frank!" and again, but louder,

IT HAPPENS TO THEM SOMETIMES

"Frank!" He was stunned for a moment and then he made himself dream that it was his wife, who stood in the field, shouting to find him. He was shaken.

"You've been sleeping for two hours," his wife explained.

He didn't catch what she'd said and he looked up at her with all his confusion exposed on his face.

"You wanted me to wake you."

He shook his head, trying to clear it, and looked back up. "I was dreaming," he told his wife.

She turned away without answering and went back into the kitchen. "It's after two," she shouted, taking the same seat she had sat in before she got up to wake him, the one beside the kitchen table. She had just finished cleaning the kitchen, wiping down the table and counters, and before that she had washed the dishes from lunch. She took a cigarette from her husband's pack and lighted it, taking a deep drag and holding the smoke before she exhaled slowly, allowing the tension to drain from her body.

Her husband appeared in the doorway, still groggy, and he plopped down in the chair closest to the living room. It was where he always sat to put his shoes on and where he sat to take them off before going into the living room to lie down on the shag-carpeted floor with his favorite turtle-shaped pillow stuffed behind his neck. One by one he slipped his black patent-leather shoes on, remembering not to lace them too tight so his feet wouldn't ache. When he finished, he dragged himself over to the counter beside the kitchen sink to get his revolver and radio. The pin, which held the cylinder of his revolver in place, had been pulled and the cartridges lay out so the bullets wouldn't accidentally trigger. It was the way he'd always left the revolver in the house, and he had developed the habit of leaving it on the counter, instead of locked in his dresser drawer, ever since his sixth and last child had gotten married and moved out. The phone, hanging on the wall above the counter, stared at him and he thought to ask his wife if anyone had called from the station, but he didn't. He didn't want her to know there was any reason for the station to be calling.

"What do you want for dinner?" his wife asked.

"I'll pick some cold cuts up from Mendini's. Don't cook. It's a hundred degrees out."

"I don't mind. I'm in the mood to cook," she lied. Really she was tired and groggy from going in and out of the house. It was so muggy and hot outside that whenever she came into the air-conditioned house, the cool, dry air gave her a headache and made her lower back stiff, or maybe it was the climbing of the stairs that stiffened her back, but either way she wearied.

"I'll pick some cold cuts up," he insisted. "I have a taste for Sorrentino's peppers. I love his peppers on sandwiches."

"We'd better ration 'em," his wife warned.

"Ration what?"

"The peppers. Mr. Sorrentino's eighty-one. We can't expect him to keep growing peppers."

"We're all old. We just work because it's who we are."

"You can only work for so long, then the body gives out."

The man grumbled and thought, the spirit gives out too, and often before the body. You should die when the spirit gives out, he thought, not when the body does.

He moved towards the table and grabbed the keys to the squad that was parked out front. It was time to move it; people complained when they saw one parked in front of a residence for too long. He left the flat, closing the door to the porch in order to keep the cooler air inside, but he left the front door ajar.

The woman heard the familiar sounds of his footsteps on the stairs and she paused to visualize his movements. She could not only tell when it was him on the stairs, but she could remember every walk her husband used from the time she had first met him on the school yard of Washington High School, shortly before he went into the army during peace time, before the Second World War. It was easy for her to recognize his walks because her husband had never thought about how he walked but instead walked the way that came naturally. She never realized she had seen something she liked in his first walk, the quick one where he kept his head raised and straight, always walking directly to his destination, and she didn't understand now that his strolling manner of walking suggested so much about his personality. She only knew that it belonged to him as uniquely as his face did.

When she heard the squad door slam, she got up and went to the freezer and shuffled through the packages of frozen meat until she found four pork chops. The meat was neatly wrapped, first in wax paper, then in cellophane, then in tin foil and finally placed in a freezer bag with a piece of loose-leaf paper taped to it, reading, "Four pork chops 6/1/79." They were just a month old. Her husband should enjoy them. "It won't be long till I'm unable to cook for him," she said to herself. "How fast time moves. Someone should have warned me. No one ever warns you how fast time moves. Boy oh boy."

She took the package to the sink and placed the plastic bag in a pot of cool water. She wanted the meat to thaw quickly so they could have the pork chops for dinner. They could have cold cuts tomorrow or for lunches.

Out of a loyalty that had long since become a habit and an accepted way of life, she had decided to do something to make her husband's life easier. She had misinterpreted his somberness. She knew about the position that had opened at the Rosewood Police Department and when her husband didn't say anything about it, she assumed it had already been filled. How could she blame him for not wanting to disappoint her again? In the thirty-eight years her husband had served the force, he had never once been promoted.

She had learned a long time ago to call her friend, Cami, to find out what was going on at the station. Cami was married to her husband's best friend, Michael Ross. Michael was only thirty-nine, but unlike Frank, he had done well for himself at the department. When he wanted to become a detective, he became one the very next month, and by the end of his fifth year, he had made sergeant.

Times were different when Michael Ross joined the force. It was a time that when you scored the highest mark on the sergeant's written exam, you would score well on the oral portion too and be next in line for promotion. Not like when Frank was Michael's age. Frank had once scored a ninety-five on the written exam, fifteen points higher than anyone in the department, but that same year he'd only scored a sixty-three on the oral portion, allowing three men to have overall scores higher than his. After that, Frank never took another exam.

But not as much corruption was tolerated by the time Michael Ross joined the force, not even in the smaller circles, because there were too many men willing to notify the state of unfair practices and no way to control them all. It was a time when the state threatened to withhold funds from the town if the police and fire departments didn't hire at least two minorities and two women in each department.

When Frank first started, there were only a few men willing to rock the boat, and it was only a matter of getting dirt on them to keep them in line. Officer Carl Lupo cheated on his wife in the early years of his marriage and the department found out about it to keep him quiet. Officer Bart Mannella filed a false theft report once so his friend could recoup his losses for the car he'd bought that turned out to be a lemon, and the department discovered this, too, by bribing one of Mannella's fellow detectives to snoop on him.

The department never bothered to get any dirt on Frank since they were able to pass him over for many promotions because Frank always bit the bullet and kept quiet. Even though Frank was sure he was more qualified than most of the mayor's friends who got promoted above him, he was never sure if he was the most qualified and he'd rather go without promotion than to have his friends think he was kissing up to the mayor and his cronies. It was his stubborn pride and the fact that money wasn't top on his priority list that kept Frank down. Not even Frank himself would deny that.

By force of habit, when Frank left his house he drove to Manny's Grill on Route 20 to get two large cups of coffee before driving over to Soscia's Auto Shop. Old man Soscia would be there even though he rarely worked on cars any longer, except for his friends' cars and the occasional smaller jobs like an oil change when the shop was especially busy. Soscia had a paranoia about the younger generation lacking integrity and he went into the shop everyday to make sure his mechanics weren't robbing him blind. When he spotted Frank passing by in the squad, he opened the rear garage door that accessed the alley, and Frank drove around and in. Soscia moved over to the pressure valve and waited for the squad to stop so he could hydraulically lift it.

"To hell with it today," Frank said. "Let 'em think what they want. I don't give a damn."

Soscia ignored him and kicked the legs of the lift into place without having to bend down and find the Chevy's frame. He lifted the car a foot off the ground, and the compressor started up so he couldn't hear Frank grumble, "Don't bother." Soscia knew that Frank had to record the squad's mileage everyday and he didn't want him to have any extra trouble at the department. Frank was on patrol and was supposed to be cruising the neighborhood, so Soscia put the car in drive and pressed a brick against the corner of the accelerator to record some miles, making it appear that Frank had been cruising the neighborhood. An hour was usually enough, recording about fifty miles.

"I told you to hell with it," Frank shouted when the compressor shut down.

"You might as well waste their gas," Soscia answered. "All the less for them to steal."

Frank grumbled something and stopped fussing. He brought the brown paper bag with the coffees into Soscia's office and he sat beside the fold-up table. The Cubs were playing the Cardinals on the small black and white but Frank didn't care much for baseball so he grabbed the deck of cards off the table and started shuffling. Soscia came in after, and Frank asked, "Gin?"

"Fine," Soscia answered, opening the bag to get the coffees out. He pulled back the plastic covers to let the coffees cool and then he gave one to Frank. They both drank their coffee black.

"You're late," Soscia said.

"Fell asleep."

"Hmm."

Frank dealt ten cards apiece and then picked up his coffee before looking at his cards.

"Did you take the promotion?" Soscia asked.

"What promotion?"

Soscia got annoyed and stared at Frank, waiting for him to come around.

"It's no promotion."

"Well, did you take it?"

"I told 'em I wasn't sure."

"Don't you want it?"

"It doesn't make much difference to me."

"But what about the money, Frank? You can always use the extra money."

"There's no difference in pay. It's just a cushier job."

"But you'll be off rotation."

"Yeah. I guess that would be good."

Being off rotation meant Frank would have regular hours that wouldn't change from month to month. As an officer at the Rosewood Police Department, you would work from eight in the morning to four in the afternoon for one month, then from four to midnight the following month and from midnight to eight the third month, before you'd start repeating.

"I'd be permanent four to twelve," Frank explained.

"You'd prefer the mornings?" Soscia asked.

"No. I like four to twelve."

"So why don't you take it?"

"I don't want to give the commander the satisfaction. He thinks he's doin' me a big favor. Him and the mayor think they can make up for thirty-eight years of bullshit."

"Fuck them. What do you care what they think?"

"I don't. What makes you think I give a shit what they think. It's what I think."

"Then take the job, if you want it."

"I might. I haven't thought much about it yet."

"When do they want to know?"

"They didn't say. I'll probably let them know today, when I go in."

"Take it if you want, Frank. To hell with what they think. You'll know."

"Yeah, I'll know. No one else will, but I'll know. To hell with them."

Frank picked up his cards. He didn't want to think about the decision anymore. Really he hadn't thought much about it at all. He just thought about it long enough to remember not to tell his wife before he gave his decision. He didn't want her to worry.

"Let's play cards," Frank said, pairing the cards in his hand. "I don't have much time. I have to stop over at Mendini's for some cold cuts before I go in."

Soscia nodded and they both went quiet. The two old men enjoyed each other's company. They could comfortably remain together in silence. At their age and living in the same town for their entire lives, there was little new to talk about, and any news that did occur in town was often the same news only happening to different people.

ဢ ಜ ಆ ဢ ಜ

At the station Frank parked the squad in the rear lot and went into the station through the back door so he wouldn't have to pass the commander's office. He brought his squad report to the front desk, carrying along a brown paper bag with cold cuts. Charlie Dimayo was working the desk, as he did Monday through Friday from eight to four, and Frank only saw him every third month when he worked the same hours on rotation.

"What do you got left?" Frank asked him.

"Two months, Frank. Two months and I'm gone."

"Thirty years."

"Yeah, thirty years, just like that, and without any memories."

"You're better off that way. Don't give them the satisfaction."

"I don't know if it's that, Frank. There's just not much to remember about this place."

"There's a few things I'll never forget."

Charlie leaned over and whispered, "Here comes the commander."

"Yeah. I know what he wants."

"What?"

"To clear his conscience."

Charlie laughed and then straightened up when the commander arrived. Charlie understood what Frank meant. Everyone in the department had been joking about the commander for the last six months, ever since he became a born-again Christian. The commander, unlike the mayor and police chief, who were middle-aged, was nearly Frank's age. He was winding down fast and did everything he could to make amends with his officers. He had been thinking about the inevitable ever since his doctor discovered a malignant tumor in his prostate. His doctor was convinced that the tumor was in remission and most likely wouldn't cause the commander's death, but it was the presence of mortality that ate away at the commander, especially in the mornings after coffee when his regular system called him to the toilet to relieve himself. The idea of death gnawed at the commander, with the only relief coming from his work.

The commander turned toward Frank. "You're in a little early," he said. "Good."

Frank peeked up from the squad report and looked the commander in the eye. "Commander."

"Can you come into my office, Frank? It'll only take a minute."

"Sure," he mumbled, "I'll be in as soon as I'm finished here."

The commander didn't hear.

"He'll be right in," said Charlie. "He's got to sign over his squad report."

The commander smiled and said, "Fine. I'll be in my office."

The commander waited for a response, but when there wasn't one, he turned and walked back to his office.

"Is it about the opening?" Charlie asked.

"Yeah."

"You gonna take it?"

"I don't know. Haven't thought about it."

"You should. Juvenile's a good spot. Everyone's bucking for it."

"I know."

"I wish it would have opened before I got behind this desk. You hear all the bitching and moaning back here. It's worse than on the street. Here we get all the crackpots. People think this is the mayor's office. You can call to complain about anything. They call on the emergency line, too. I had a broad today, on the emergency line, bitching about a pothole in front of her driveway."

Frank nodded. "Thirty-eight years I've been here. There ain't nothin' I haven't heard."

"I know, Frank. So do yourself a favor and take the position. If you're going for forty years, you might as well make it easy on yourself."

"You don't have to worry about that. I decided that a long time ago. Since the last time I took the sergeant's exam,

84

almost twenty years ago. And even before that, now that I think about it."

"Good," Charlie said. "That's good to hear. You deserve it more than anyone."

Frank signed the squad car report and left for the commander's office. When he walked in, the commander asked him to shut the door.

"I've got nothing to hide," Frank said, taking a seat across the desk from the commander, who was sitting on the edge of his large leather swivel chair.

"If you prefer it that way, that's fine."

"I don't talk behind closed doors."

"That's fine, Frank. It's just about the position in juvenile. Everyone knows I've offered it to you."

"I guess they do."

"So what do you say? Would you like it?"

"Did you check with the mayor?"

"Come on, Frank. You know he doesn't have his hands in this."

"Yeah, you're right. It's too small time."

"Take the spot. You've only got two years left."

"Two years is a long time for someone like me."

"I know. That's why I'm offering you this. It'll make it easier for you."

"Easier for me or for you?"

"For you, Frank. I'm doin' this for you."

"You really want to make things easier for me?"

"Sure. You know that."

"You got anyone in mind to work the desk when Charlie's gone?"

"Not really, I thought we'd hire someone temporarily, not police personnel. Leave the desk open in case anyone gets hurt, and we need a soft job . . . Why?"

"Would you let me take over when he's gone?"

"The desk?"

"Yeah."

"But that's a shit job, Frank. Why would you want that?"

"You said you wanted to make it easier on me."

"I do. But are you sure that's what you want?"

"That's what I want."

"I wish you'd let me help you out. Make it easy on yourself."

"That's just what I'm doin'. That's what I've done for the last forty years."

The commander sighed. "You're as stubborn as a mule."

"Is that all?"

"If you're sure you don't want the juvenile spot."

"Who's next in line for it?"

"I was thinking about Sam Toscano."

"Good. Give it to Sammy. Tell him it's an anniversary present from me. Fourteen years here is as good as forever."

Frank walked out of the commander's office and didn't look around to see who was watching him come out, he just turned and walked out the front door. It was the first time he had gone through the front door in his thirty-eight years on the force. He had to walk around the building to the parking lot where he had parked his car. It was only five blocks to his house but he had been taking the car ever since his wife had decided she could no longer drive.

At the house he parked the car in the garage and his wife didn't hear him pull in because the air conditioner was on high. It was nearly a hundred degrees outside and having the air on only made it bearable up on the second floor, especially with the stove on. His wife didn't hear him coming up the stairs, nor walking through the open porch door.

Suddenly she heard whistling coming from the porch and she opened the inside door to find her husband sitting down, taking his shoes off.

"What are you doing?" she asked.

"Taking my shoes off."

"Out here?"

"Sure. Why not?"

"I don't know. You just never do it out here."

"There's a lot of things I've never done. But I'm not against them all. I just don't think about it much."

"What's this nonsense?"

"It's not nonsense."

"Well, come on in. It's boiling out here, and dinner's almost ready."

"I brought cold cuts."

"That's OK. We can have 'em for lunch tomorrow. I made pork chops."

"Are you crazy? It's a hundred degrees outside!"

"They're breaded and fried. I didn't bake 'em."

"Still, you gotta be crazy."

"It's this house. It makes us all crazy."

Frank laughed and he did something that he hadn't done in a long time. He wondered what his wife was thinking. He had been struggling for so long, ever since he was nineteen, that he had accepted his own reasons for everything his wife did. But today she was on his mind and he wondered why she would have thought to cook pork chops.

"You must have heard," he said.

"Cami told me."

"I wish she hadn't."

"You've got nothing to be embarrassed about. You should be proud that you haven't stooped to their level."

Frank paused. "What have you heard?"

"About the promotion to the juvenile position. I'm sorry you didn't get it."

"How did you know I didn't take it?"

"I thought when you were quiet today, that they gave it to someone else."

"No. They offered it to me. Is that why you cooked the pork chops, to cheer me up?"

"I guess. Well, now it'll be to celebrate. That's wonderful."

87

"Yeah. We can celebrate. I didn't take it."

"What do you mean?"

"Just what I said. I didn't take it."

"But why?"

"Didn't want it."

His wife became so confused that she couldn't say anything at first and then she asked, "Did you quit? I wouldn't blame you if you quit. You don't have to worry about the extra pension. We'll manage."

"I didn't quit."

"But you said we should celebrate. If you didn't retire, what are we celebrating?"

"My death."

"Don't talk silly."

"I'm not."

"Why don't you just retire early? If you're tired of the department, you should just retire. You've put in thirty-eight years. That's plenty."

"Thirty-eight years and I'll put in two more, too, if I don't die first. It's the same as it's always been. It just took me thirty-eight years to see it. I could work there 'til I die if I had to."

"So what's all this silly talk about celebrating your death?"

"When it comes, it'll be a peaceful one."

"I don't understand."

"The mayor and I aren't so different," he said, rumbling with laughter, making his wife think he had gone mad.

"I finally realized something," he continued. "I had a dream about it this afternoon but I didn't figure it out until just now. I'm everyone and I'm myself. I'm not going to let the mayor get to me anymore. Don't you see? I understand him now. He's a lot like me. We both live our lives to make things easier on ourselves. The only difference is that I live my life to make my death a peaceful one, and he lives his to make his life more comfortable. Other than that, we're really just the same."

A Generation of Mavericks

CLUB FLEXIBLE WAS LOCATED INSIDE A gutted-out shoe factory and its entranceway gave access to the alley that ran along the Lincoln Avenue "el" tracks. Since its opening, the club had seen two drug busts and several brawls and the owner spent little money on decor. The inside walls had been plastered over and painted a dull gray and you could easily camouflage yourself by wearing dark clothing and standing still along the edges. Several times throughout the night, vapors would pour out onto the dance floor filling the room with fog and making it impossible to see things clearly. If you went dancing, though, the faces of everyone around you glowed a bright white from the track lighting mounted above and you could see the reflections of anyone wearing metal chains around their boots.

It was a risky club to visit alone but it was safe to go with friends. In the back the men would meet to tell stories of fallen women and victorious brawls they had had and if you remained quiet against the far wall you could get close enough to hear them hoot and call out to the women on the dance floor. It would have been easy to make fun of them, but you'd be pressed to find anyone doing it. In large groups the men became more reckless and cruel and everyone kept a wary eye on them. But if you kept to yourself and wore inconspicuous, dark clothing there was little chance you'd be noticed. It was generally the naive or the newcomers who were at risk.

A young man named Peter Wiley, who often went out alone, was fond of the club and he visited almost every Thursday for ladies' night. He felt comfortable standing among the different groups and with time he had forgotten he wasn't friends with any of them. He had been going out alone for several years now and had developed certain habits that become as important to him as decision-making. Peter Wiley would no sooner strip naked than take a different spot against the back wall.

Sometimes he would stand alone for hours waiting for a woman to wander back alone, late at night, when she was drunk, or in a friendly mood, or perhaps unaware of the danger. Or he would wait for a group of women to wander back, but mostly they mingled in front near the bar where they waited for someone to buy them a drink or proposition them to dance. The club was a pickup joint. Neither the men nor the women who visited possessed much character.

Peter Wiley had watched these women, though, for a long time and he could tell from the way they walked and talked whether or not they wanted to be approached. At times he had gotten caught up with some. He had fed certain ones a line and played along with their games of seduction. He had even dated some and felt disgust towards himself and them knowing he could win their favor dishonestly. Still, he had always hoped he'd approach a woman who would catch him playing the game and demand more from him. He was convinced he could fall in love with such a woman.

He continued to visit the club for that reason and it became as much a home to him as it was a hangout, built there for him to go and find his way through times of indecision. He liked that the club was always kept dark with the exception of the recurring flashes of the strobe lights. It was much further west than most other clubs in Chicago and far away from the well-to-do neighborhoods. Not until after midnight would it become busy and then if you were tall enough you would see nothing but heads for several hours until the club started to thin again at two or three in the morning.

When it drew towards midnight, Peter Wiley sunk further into the back corner and rested his arm on the ledge that ran along the side wall. He had his draught beer with him that had been poured into a chilled mug and the condensed water had formed into slush and slid off the mug in clumps to land on the ledge where it rested. He never took his hand off the mug and it was as much a part of his visits as was admiring the sights. He knew that soon the club would get hot and his mug would become even more important. He liked to run it across his forehead and along his face and down into the front of his shirt. Putting the mug down his shirt excited him as much as it cooled him and he always looked down when he did it and only wondered if any of the women took interest.

After a first beer he had a tall whiskey and soda and the waitress knew to bring it with a large straw. Close up the clear liquid glowed in his hand underneath the purple light and he watched as the carbonation rose to the surface. He knew it was a bad idea to drink distills, seeing that he drank often, but he was tired of the taste of beer and a light whiskey and soda was more refreshing.

Standing in the cove he could feel a gentle breeze coming from the ventilation shaft some fifteen feet above and he wondered when it would get too crowded to tell if the fan was on. He could feel the vibrations of the speakers which hung down from the ceiling and vibrated the wall behind him.

He knew he wouldn't come if it weren't for the music and he listened to it gratefully and thought of how it would be to go home and play his favorite songs. The nights were his favorite times in the city and he labored through the days to get to every one of them.

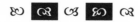

The day was over and it was well into the night so that there were women gathered at the bar, and many were dancing with other women and men. The crowd was growing fast and the front door remained open, where a man with a flashlight sat outside on a stool checking identifications and charging only the men five dollars to enter. The flow of the crowd split at the edge of the dance floor, and the strobe light flickered, making the motion of the people appear slower than it really was, as everyone hurried in to find their spots against the railing that surrounded the sunken dance floor. On top of the railing there were drinks rested on napkins, threatening to fall over onto the dancers, and a bouncer walked around asking people to remove them and taking the ones that no one claimed.

A woman stood alone alongside the railing with her thin fingers wrapped around a tall vodka collins that she held at her waist, and she looked around the room confidently as if she were making a determination about every patron. She took a measured sip from her cocktail and blew out through her thin pressed lips to keep her teeth from aching cold, and Peter Wiley slid to his right so that he could get a full view of her from across the dance floor. He had to move from behind the tall woman wearing a pair of skin-tight stirrups and the three aging boys who had gathered around to admire the pants.

Peter was accustomed to watch for the same few women who frequented the club, whom he liked to muse about from afar, and he was surprised to see someone new who could seize his attention so easily. It was a refreshing change, he thought, that came when he was about to give up seeing anyone he knew. Otherwise he was familiar with his routine visits, where he would stand in the back alone for hours, waiting to see someone familiar so that when he approached his need to socialize wouldn't be taken as a pass. It brought him much pain to be misunderstood and it was quite often that he'd remained at the club for an entire night without speaking to anyone besides the waitress when he ordered his drinks. Sometimes it was only the few people around him who knew he was there. Even when he went to the bathroom, he put his head down and walked quickly, only to return to the same spot the same way. He would never place himself on display unless he was in control. He knew that a humbling experience would be devastating at a time when he lacked direction.

But he was determined to approach someone tonight, within the restraints of his self-indulgent integrity, and he made a serious effort to find any reason he could to convince himself that this woman would be different. When the strobe flashed again it gave him a better glimpse of her and he could see that she was beautiful, with wide round eyes and a thin nose. She stood beside the three-step stairway that led down onto the dance floor, and her body remained still with only her eyes moving. She stands just like me, he thought.

"Do you always come out alone?" he imagined he would ask.

"Oh, I'm impressed," she might reply, sarcastically of course. "What an inventive come-on."

"Fine, then. I should have known better. Why should you be any different? They're all the same here. They're all the same everywhere."

"Really?"

"Yes, really!" he would snap back, and then stop to ponder his comments and thoughts, until he would feel confident enough to continue. "Well, maybe there are two types of people here. The ones who have nothing to offer but act like they do, and the ones who have nothing to offer and admit that they don't. Either way I lose."

"And what about you? Where do you fit in?"

"I don't know . . . With the bitter ones, I guess. How would you feel if there were only two groups of people here and you didn't fit in with either?"

She looks around the room. "Here?" she asks. "Then why don't you go somewhere else?"

"There is nowhere else. Not for me, not now . . . What about you? Why do you come here? Don't you have any need to socialize? How can anyone not need to socialize, when not being able to makes me so miserable."

The woman didn't answer.

"That's why I came up to you. You were alone. I was kind of hoping you might be like me. That is, in the same situation. But from your reaction, I guess I was wrong."

He turns and starts walking back to the corner of the room.

"No wait," the woman says. "You're kind of cute."

"Cute?!"

"Please," she sighs. "There's no need to nitpick at my word choice. And I wasn't being conceited before. I was being cautious. This isn't the best place to meet someone."

"No. I guess it's not."

He had opened his eyes and his vision adjusted to the darkness of the corner where he had been dreaming and he looked out across the dance floor and found the woman still standing there, unladylike, as women sometimes did when they appeared in classic movies and played opposite roles to wise guys, and she was like no woman that Peter Wiley had ever known except for maybe Michelle Pfieffer. Of course, Peter Wiley didn't know the real Michelle Pfieffer but thought only of her role as the mistress to Al Pacino in *Scarface*, where she was always confident and in control of all the people around her and knowing what each person wanted from her and what she wanted from them.

She doesn't look conceited, he thought, quiet and discreet. "Or maybe I'm just drunk," he mumbled to himself and then lifted his mug off the ledge and took a sip of beer.

He knew she wouldn't remain there for long and he thought of other things that might coax him to approach. It used to be easy to approach women when he was in college. He would just think of something to say and then go over and say it, but now he knew more about human nature and as soon as he thought of something to say he would conceive an unfavorable response. It might be easy though, he thought. How hard could it be to impress someone here?

The cocktail waitress broke through the crowd and into the corner, where she whirled around so that her back faced the wall, and then she fell backwards and sighed, "Phew," as she bounced off the wall.

"How's it going?" he asked.

"I'm beat," the waitress blurted, with her breath escaping her along with her words. "I wanna get out of here."

"You better slow down. You're going to knock yourself out."

"I know. I know. It's always busy like this."

The waitress ran her fingers nervously along the pleats in her vintage skirt and her long nails scraped into the wool fibers.

"I like the skirt," he said.

"Really?" the waitress asked gleefully. "It's too long though. It rubs against the floor when I don't stand right."

"But it looks good. I like that it's long. It hangs well."

"Thanks, Peter. You're always so nice."

"Nice? Not really. In fact I'm almost never nice. There's always a reason why I do things."

"Don't talk silly."

He mumbled, "I didn't think I was."

"What?"

"Nothing. Don't worry about it. Are you going to take a break?"

"I can't. It's too busy. I'm looking for Michael though. Did you see him?"

"Michael?"

"You know, Michael," the waitress said, motioning to her nose.

"No. I didn't. But you should stay away from that stuff."

"I know. It's terrible, isn't it? It keeps me thin though. You want another beer?"

"Sure. But get it later. Take a break."

"No. I'd better keep moving."

"Let me buy us a shot then."

"Later maybe. Bobby gets ticked if we drink too early. You want one?"

"No. Just a beer."

"OK."

The waitress arched her back and rose off the wall, and Peter watched her rush towards the front bar until she disappeared into the crowd where the people, now jammed together, moved like water and filled the void after she had gone through.

The dance floor was crowded too and he looked around, searching for anyone with the same long, brown hair as the woman had had across the room. I should have gone up to her, he thought. I shouldn't have waited so long. I always wait too long. "Ah, the hell with it," he grumbled. "It would have never happened. I'd have never gone up to her. I couldn't have. I'm not lonely enough." And he took another sip of beer and laid the near-empty mug on the ledge beside him.

The same feeling he had felt the previous week when he visited returned to the pit of his stomach and he felt the fatigue of the depressed so he gulped the last of his beer and started to think of what liquor he would shoot. He knew the only thing that pleased him anymore was that he could manage alone indefinitely and he didn't like much of anything except the satisfaction of knowing he wasn't hypocritical with his feelings like many people he knew. Or at least he hadn't been lately.

He stared vaguely, facing the dance floor, and was completely amazed at how empty a crowded room could seem at times, and the music became that much more vital. Sometimes when he was watching people he wasn't aware of how important the music was, but he knew then the comfort it added to anyone who ventured out alone. It removed the pressure which was placed on him by the eyes watching and wondering why he wasn't socializing since most of the people who came in groups remained silent also because it was often too loud to talk.

Numbness ran through his body as he mouthed the words to the Cure's song that was playing. He was particularly fond of the song but not of all progressive music. Mostly it was the erratic tempo he liked because it absorbed his tensions.

He felt tired and looked around the room, trying not to focus on anything, but he couldn't help but notice the gaudy, obvious man talking at the two ladies. The man laughed with ease and that annoyed him. He noticed the man's clothes too and thought of how silly the man looked: a sleeveless shirt in October!

His face flushed. He couldn't help but feel frustration now and he thought of shoving his fist down the man's throat. I could get away with it, he thought. Two quick punches to flatten the guy and then take off for the door.

Maybe I could rid the world of a little conceit, he thought. This guy thinks that because he doesn't know what he's doing, no one else can figure it out?! Maybe I'll compile a huge list of all the stupid reasons people do things so at least people will be humble. Ah, who am I kidding? They'll never be humble. It's not in the order of things. I'll just flatten him!

The disc jockey mixed a new song in with the end of another and Peter Wiley lost his concentration for the moment and then wondered where his beer was. He looked around and when he spotted the cocktail waitress across the room he followed her with his eyes until she was in front of him with her tray. He grabbed the mug off with no need to ask the price. It was two-fifty and he handed her a five as usual not expecting any change.

"Thanks, Peter," the waitress said and then leaned over and kissed him softly on the cheek.

"It's nothing. I don't care about money."

"God, I'm exhausted," she said. "I'm glad it's finally slowing."

"Good. Then can we do a shot?"

"Sure. But Bobby's buying. I owe you one."

"What do you want?" he asked.

"How 'bout Jagermeister?"

"Too sweet. How about Blanton's?"

"Sure. That's fine."

"But let's get snifters and sip them. I hate them damn plastic shot glasses."

"Of course, Peter. I take care of my good customers. You won't go anywhere?"

He smiled. "No. I won't go anywhere. Just hurry. I need a shot."

When the waitress was out of sight, Peter reached into his coat pocket for his pen and then he took the napkin, which was damp in spots, off the ledge and did his best to write on the dry spaces.

"It's becoming harder and harder for me to find something to amuse me," he wrote. He liked to keep some record of his time spent in clubs or else it would be a complete loss. He finished with, "The immensity of a delusion necessary to support a liaison with most people is becoming absurd." He shoved the napkin in his pocket. I'll just have a few drinks, he decided. I don't want falling asleep to be a challenge. He stood for several minutes with his eyes focused on the floor before someone approached.

Peter Wiley had had his head down when she approached, and on the floor in front of him was a pair of cumbersome black shoes staring up at him. The woman had already greeted him once but when there was no response she stood waiting patiently with both her hands on her hips. He could see the bottom of her multicolored skirt flowing underneath the ventilation shaft and he could smell and hear her braided hair when she threw it back over her shoulder.

She was a voluptuous woman, he knew, but no one else could tell because the woman had covered her body underneath layers of baggy clothing. She wasn't very pretty, though, but she had certain pleasing features being blessed with large, round eyes and full lips and he got the feeling that she could have easily done better with men if she didn't conceal her figure. It was only her clothes that made her appear heavy.

"Well, how are you?" the woman persisted, and Peter finally looked up to see the fading patches of freckles on her almost round face.

"How do I look?"

"You look great. Why?"

"I don't feel great. I feel like shit."

"I guess you still haven't found what you're looking for. Have you?"

"No. I haven't."

"That's OK, Peter. I wouldn't have expected you to. That's why I like talking with you."

"I feel like an idiot. I am an idiot. I'm not even sure why I come here anymore. Somewhere in the back of my mind is this idea that someone will finally come here for the same reasons I do, and everything will be fine. But I never find anyone."

He stopped to sip some beer, it was still very cold and the second gulp was more refreshing then the first.

"All I find here are a bunch of sluts who paint their pants on and these idiot guys chasing them around. The funniest thing is that this place is the least offensive place I can find. At least here there are some people who are so fucked up that it's impossible to figure them out. Not like some places. Some places you don't even have to look around to tell what the people are like. They're all the same."

The woman laughed, "I'm glad you haven't changed much."

Good old Francine, he thought, I'll never scare her away. He didn't bother to look her in the eyes so she remained unaware of her effect on him. He allowed some of the tension in his muscles to drain, and as the blood rushed through his veins he felt the urge to smile but resisted.

"What have you been up to?" he asked.

"Nothing much. I went to class tonight. Do you like the blouse? I made it."

"It's certainly you. Lots of dark colors."

"Is that good?"

"I don't know. Why?"

"Because I want to know what you think."

"But I don't know anything about fashion."

"So?"

"Well, your opinion's the only one that matters."

"But I'm not like you, Peter. Your opinion matters to me."

"It's a nice blouse already. I didn't mean to make a fuss about it."

"Thanks," she said, smiling as if she had accomplished some victory.

The waitress returned to the corner with two snifters of Blanton's and she held them in her left hand with the two stems between her fingers.

"Kelly, this is Francine."

"Hi," the women said simultaneously.

"What should we drink to?" Peter asked. "You can have some of mine," he said to Francine.

"Let's drink to getting out of here," said Kelly.

"Sounds good to me."

The two drank from their snifters and Kelly finished her bourbon in two swallows while Peter sipped a bit and then passed the snifter to Francine.

"Thanks, Kelly."

"Don't worry about it. Maybe we'll do another later. Nice meeting you," she said and then left for the bar. When she was out of audible range Francine asked, "Who's she?"

"I just know her from here. She buys me a drink now and then. But I tip the hell out of her. Or at least better than most."

"Am I going to get you in trouble?"

"She has a boyfriend. She's nothing to me. She's kind of flaky too. I don't think I'd have the patience."

"Good."

"What about you? I haven't seen you in a while."

"I don't know. Just roaming. You know me."

"No new boyfriends?"

"No."

"They're idiots, that's why. They don't know what's good for them."

"Maybe."

"Of course they are. Just like the guys here."

"You're here."

"I know. I shouldn't be. You want to take a walk? I've tortured myself long enough. I'm ready to get out of here."

"I've got a couple of roaches. We can get high."

"Sure. I haven't gotten high in a while."

"Just don't get me in trouble again," she teased.

"What? You don't have to come if you don't want."

"I'll come. It's just every time we're together, I wind up wasted. You always make me drink too much."

"Oh, that. That's OK. It's good to get wasted once in a while. Sometimes I even get the feeling I've accomplished something when I've gotten really wasted . . . Come on," he said, reaching out his hand.

Francine followed as he wove a path through the crowded room and she felt special holding his hand for it wasn't often they did, and that made the simple pleasure more pleasurable, and she looked around the room noticing the envious people watching them leave. She thought Peter was a striking man, tall and stern with a handsome facial structure. She never thought of his face as contorted or thin as some did, nor did she notice the shadows that his contortions produced. She did everything she could to keep up with his pace and when his overcoat flew in the breeze, she smiled.

Through the door, they fell out into the gangway that led to the street and walked north along Lincoln Avenue.

Francine knew where she was going and she led them to a nearby parking lot which was trapped between two buildings and an alley.

The cool October air lightened Peter's head and he pulled Francine into a doorjamb on the side of the southernmost building. They were no longer visible to the street and he started fondling her breasts and buttocks while he kissed her.

"I wanna eat you up," he said, nibbling on her neck and tasting the sweet essences of her body. "You're delicious."

"You're tickling."

"You want me to stop?"

"No! Not at all. But how come you're being so friendly today?"

"Let's just say I'm glad to see you. I've had a bad day."

"I wish you were always this glad to see me," she said, falling deeper into his arms. She loved everything about him. She hugged him hard for a moment and then reached into her suede jacket pocket for a roach. From behind his head she lit it and took a deep drag, holding the smoke for as long as she could, and then she tilted her head back and pressed her lips to his. She blew the smoke into his mouth and he tried to hold it, but he couldn't keep from coughing.

"Are you OK?" she asked, laughing at his novice effort.

"Yes. You just blew the smoke too fast," he said and then forced himself to cough again, and then again.

"Here," she said, passing the joint, and when he stopped coughing he took a slow, steady drag and immediately felt the effects. He passed the joint back to her, and she to him, and with every drag she felt more relaxed and pleased, and he felt less of everything but tired. They finished the roach and another half a joint before she took him by the hand and guided him out of the lot.

Without any discussion they started walking up Lincoln Avenue. They stumbled along the street like two newborn fawns taking their first steps and their pace was less than half of what a sober couple's might have been. In anyone else's eye they might have appeared unfortunate holding each other up, but they didn't care. They never measured their relative misfortune. They looked at life as life and took their steps slowly.

ৡ ** স** ৩ **ৡ** স

It took them nearly twenty minutes to walk the four and a half blocks to Francine's apartment and there had been no conversation along the way. They stood outside her front door and Peter smelled an unfamiliar stench in the hallway and looked down to see the heavily stained carpet.

"I've got to pee bad," Fran said, rubbing her thighs back and forth.

"Well, hurry."

"I am. I am."

"You're lucky you don't have a combination lock. You'd never get in."

"Shut up, silly. I got to go bad."

She continued to fumble through her jacket pockets, looking desperately for her keys, and then she dropped the key ring as soon as she produced it. She giggled uncomfortably for a moment and when she saw that Peter wasn't watching, she stooped down to get it and then unlocked the door quickly and rushed into the bathroom.

Peter heard her slam the bathroom door before he stumbled in and he left the front door to close under its own weight. He didn't think to lock it and didn't notice that it remained slightly ajar. There was a mattress on the floor in the only other room besides the bathroom and he was glad to see it. His legs were killing him and after taking off his coat and tossing it over a chair, he walked over to the mattress and plopped down on the center.

It was a small room for a studio apartment with the oven, sink and mini-refrigerator offensively visible. The place was filthy, too, and not because of Fran's laziness, but from years of managerial neglect. Soot from the street had been ground into the carpet fibers and the walls and windows were covered with a thick film. Any effort to make the apartment smell pleasant would have been in vain, but it was all that Fran could afford and it wasn't a great bother to either of them.

The window above the head of the mattress was cracked and he leaned back against the wall trying to breath the cooler, untainted air as it dropped into the room. His eyes were half-closed, his head spun and he was doing all he could to sober himself. He took long, deep breaths and shook his head but it only made things worse.

"I don't remember it being so small in here," he shouted.

"What?"

"Nothing. How come you hang your clothes on the walls?"

"They're from my class."

"They make me dizzy," he said, feeling the nausea rise from his full belly, and he was relieved when she appeared from the bathroom.

"Hi," he said, smiling uncontrollably.

"You look so cute."

"Cute? I'm a mess."

"No you're not. You look good. You want me to roll us another joint?"

"If you want. I don't need any."

"OK. You'll have some. It'll make you feel nice."

"It'll make me tired."

"No it won't."

She fetched a bag of pot from the cabinet above the sink and rolled another joint before joining him. Her ashtray and lighter were already on the floor beside the mattress and when she grabbed the lighter, she pulled the ashtray closer.

He watched her take a deep drag, lighting the joint, and although he was higher than he wanted to be, he took a hit when she offered. She took a second drag and offered it back.

"No," he said. "I'm wasted."

"Are you sure?"

"Yes," and he pushed the joint away and then dropped his hand on the mattress between her legs. Leaning over, he could see her full breasts dangling low in her blouse and he started unbuttoning his shirt and then hers before he finished his own. She continued to get high, though, taking a third hit when he stood and leaned against the windowsill.

"Give me your hand," he slurred.

She did, sliding up along his body while he wrapped his arms around her hips and pulled himself into her voluptuous body. He gave her a kiss on the neck and then the collarbone, noticing that hers was curved softly unlike his own, so he bit into it with uncontrollable lust. He kissed between her breasts and then below them until he got to her waist, where he untied her skirt and let it drop to the floor. She felt the skirt over her feet and stepped out of it, never taking time away from her smoking, and she took another drag from the joint and blew the smoke towards the ceiling.

Back on the mattress he straddled over her full, rounded thighs and she leaned against the wall, wearing only the unbuttoned blouse, which had fallen from her shoulders. She wasn't wearing a bra and he licked and sucked her breasts, noticing her large brown nipples, and he ran his fingers around them before she finally reached over to extinguish the joint. Peter was very anxious to sever into Francine's flesh and he did what he could with his lips and tongue for as long as he could and he made sure to lick every erogenous part of her body, even though he spent little time anywhere, and then he undressed himself and mounted her for what he had reduced to instinct.

They were both very drunk and it was difficult to stay aroused. Francine was almost always kinky, she was almost always high, and she put her finger where she thought he might like it.

"Use your finger," she whispered. "Use your finger." And she felt the blood rush to her groin. But Peter only got the idea to place something else where she had shoved her finger and he thought about the constriction that might force an orgasm.

They both did whatever they could to get off. He pounded and pounded both of her breaches, while she furiously grinded against his pelvis. They grew sweatier and sweatier in the humid room and their chests sucked apart each time Peter arched his back. All in all they must have screwed for over fifty minutes before Peter finally rolled off and let out a long sigh. It's no use, he thought. His arms were tired and he knew no matter how hard he tried, he wasn't going to relieve himself that way.

Francine had followed him when he moved away and she watched him lie restlessly with his eyes closed.

"I can't leave you like that," she said, passing her fingers lightly over his chest. "I wish I could do something for you."

"It's me. I can't."

She watched him fidget as her mind raced through her options and then she pushed herself off the mattress and mounted him. She took it upon herself to put his penis where she assumed he wanted it most and with one last diligent effort she was able to relieve him.

That was the last thing that happened, besides a toss or a turn, before they both passed out.

Peter woke once in the early morning and found himself sobering and uncomfortable in the tiny room. He was desperate to get out of the confinement but he didn't want to deal with saying good-bye. Francine didn't expect anything from him, but he felt obligated because he knew she would have taken more if he offered.

In his mind he worked out what he would say, but he never woke her. Do you want to know something, Francine? he thought. You and I share the closest thing to a real relationship that I've ever had. I mean, we're always friends . . . we're occasionally lovers . . . and you don't ever expect anything from me. Why? You're probably the only one who deserves anything.

He gave her a kiss on the forehead and left. He wasn't ready for anything else.

Little Hands

S HE HAD SUCH LITTLE HANDS, SO SMALL THAT
anyone else who might have been endowed with them
would have complained and wondered why they were
condemned to live their lives with such tiny hands. But she
was quite content with them. She didn't need nor want big
hands. Big hands were far too dangerous. Of course, she
knew she could get her work around the house done quicker
with larger and stronger hands. But then what would she do
with herself if she finished too early, and what satisfaction
would she get from a job that she could finish quickly and
effortlessly. It scared her to death when she thought of the
cost she'd have to pay just to possess big hands. How many
heirlooms would she have broken, or dulled the shine on over
the years because of big hands that were prone to scrub too
vigorously.

No, she was happy to have her little hands and had long
since learned how to work well with them. In the cabinets
above the sink in the kitchen, you could see the evidence of
the care she took with her patient, little hands. There was not
even the slightest chip or crack on anything neatly stacked
inside, not a crack in a single crystal glass, nor a chip on a single piece of china, not even the delicate china cups that

belonged to her mother and were not only delicate but old as well. Yes, her little hands had served her well and for quite a long time.

Whenever she cleaned the dishes after dinner, she would press her four fingers together tightly, and with a napkin, she'd wipe around the edge of a plate, making large circles and then progressively smaller ones until she had wiped the plate clean, then she would take the next plate and do the same until she had emptied all the remnants of food from all the plates onto one plate, which she would then take to the garbage can and wipe clean in the same manner she had wiped the others. When she finished wiping the plates, she would carefully carry the stack over to the kitchen sink, straining all the way. There she would rinse them off before dipping them into the basin filled with soapy water.

Around the house, she always worked with great care and it often took her more than two hours to finish scrubbing the dishes after the entire family had eaten on a Sunday afternoon. It became a familiar sight to the rest of the family, seeing her there standing in front of the kitchen sink with her back to everyone. She'd spent a good portion of her life that way, which may have given the impression that she wasn't involved in the family's daily life and planning, but this was not the case. Like the rest of the family, she had disproportionately large ears and over the years her ears had bent back some so that with time she began to hear better from behind than she could from the front. She heard every word that was spoken at the kitchen table after dinner and it was only that she rarely spoke that gave some of the family members the impression that she wasn't involved in the discussions.

Every now and then, to the family's surprise, she would interject something. Most often it was in defense of the children, none of which were her own, although she thought of them that way. All the children in the family were born to her sisters, but they were loved as much by her as they were by their own mothers. She was always quick to defend the children. There was the time when the youngest girl wanted to play baseball on a local little league team. The girl was quite competitive at the time, growing up with three brothers and playing all the games they did. She didn't see why she couldn't play baseball in a league now. But the family said, "No. It isn't right. What will they think next-door?"

Then out of nowhere, the woman with the little hands spoke up. "What difference does it make what they think?" she asked.

The family was shocked at first and quick to disregard her comments. "Don't be silly," they said. "She can't play baseball. Are you crazy?"

"Why not? If it'll make her happy, why can't she play? She'd still be the same wonderful girl that she is."

The rest of the family was silent a moment and with time they began to be won over. "Maybe," they said, "it wouldn't change anything. She would still be the same sweet child." They couldn't deny that.

On many occasions the woman with the little hands fought for the children, regardless of how it might have alienated her from the rest of the family. She cared only about the children's welfare and never once thought about how her sisters might ridicule her for her comments, which were almost never popular but always needed to be said. Once, when one of the older boys decided to get an earring, the rest of the family was shocked and outraged. It was almost an assault on the family to do something as an individual without the family's approval.

But the woman with the little hands wasn't upset, and she only thought about what she could do to help the boy. She was so pleased when she remembered the diamond stud earrings, of which she had lost one. She never knew what to do with the remaining one, but now she could give it to her nephew and know it would be put to use. Such things would have never occurred to anyone else in the family, but shortly after the woman with little hands gave her diamond stud to her nephew, everyone else followed suit. All the women in the family dug out their old, single earrings and gave them to the boy, asking only that he return them if they found the missing one.

The work the woman with the little hands did around the house was enough to fill almost anyone's day, especially hers because she had to work extra hard to do the same work as someone much larger. But she was never satisfied to do just housework. She had always worked at her father's store when she was young, and after he died she took over completely. But as business went down and she grew older, she could no longer manage the store and was forced to close down the store that had personally served so many people in the constantly changing neighborhood.

For the next year, away from the daily life outside the home, she felt that a part of her self was missing. She didn't know exactly what it was, but she knew it had something to do with the store. So when a job offer came to be a clerk at the larger, local grocery store, she was quick to offer her services.

The entire family was perplexed when they heard of her decision. At her age to return to work, when she already had so much work at home and no need for the extra money, appeared foolish. They would have argued with her to the death, but she had made the decision so discreetly and so firmly that they realized there would be no use in trying to talk her out of it, although they did make disapproving comments whenever it came up. The family couldn't understand why she insisted on working. There was no reason for it.

But the woman with little hands understood, as she was quick to recall why she loved to work outside the house. Only at work did she receive the praise for the extra care she took, a care that her family enjoyed but had long since grown accustomed to. How good she felt when the man who smoked the fancy cigarettes from Britain came in and thanked her graciously when she pulled up from under the counter the carton of cigarettes that she had saved for him. How good she felt when the manager was so pleased that when times were slow, she cleaned around her register area because she'd rather work than sit around doing nothing. She wasn't much of a talker and preferred to work, but, oh, how good it made her feel to be appreciated. At home she was more likely to be looked down upon for lacking in social skills, but never at work. At work she always wore a smile and always had a kind word. She was Frances at work.

When she returned home from work, she felt refreshed and found her housework less draining. She immediately started preparing dinner and cleaning up in-between. There was always so much to do, and little time could be wasted. It was only late in the evening that she took any time at all for herself. Every day she would set her VCR to tape her favorite soap opera, *Days of Our Lives*, so she could watch it late in the evening when her long day was ending. There she would sit on the couch, exhausted but fulfilled, knowing that her little hands had accomplished so much during the day.

One day in the middle of the summer, on a hot and muggy day, she sat on the couch more exhausted than ever. She put her little hands over her exhausted heart and she felt better. Later, when she went to sleep, her hands fell off her chest without her knowing.

In the morning the family woke and at first they didn't notice that the woman with the little hands wasn't there, even though she was always up first. It wasn't until her brother went to pour himself a cup of coffee and there wasn't any brewed that the family realized that she was gone.

About the Author

Vincent Sperando was born in Chicago, Illinois in 1964 and grew up in the Italian-American suburb of Melrose Park.

He studied physics at the University of Illinois and graduated in 1987. After doing graduate work in physics, he moved to New York City to pursue his writing career. He studied creative writing at Columbia University.

Vincent now lives in Australia with his wife, where he is pursuing a degree in medicine from the University of Sydney. He is also working on a new novel which will be set in Australia.